Enjoy eight new titles from Harlequin Presents in August!

Lucy Monroe brings you her next story in the fabulous ROYAL BRIDES series, and look out for Carole Mortimer's second seductive Sicilian in her trilogy THE SICILIANS. Don't miss Miranda Lee's ruthless millionaire, Sarah Morgan's gorgeous Greek tycoon, Trish Morey's Italian boss and Jennie Lucas's forced bride! Plus, be sure to read Kate Hardy's story of passion leading to pregnancy in *One Night, One Baby,* and the fantastic *Taken by the Maverick Millionaire* by Anna Cleary!

We'd love to hear what you think about Presents. E-mail us at Presents@hmb.co.uk or join in the discussions at www.iheartpresents.com and www.sensationalromance.blogspot.com, where you'll also find more information about books and authors!

Kate Hardy

ONE NIGHT, ONE BABY

TAKEN BY THE
MILLIONAIRE

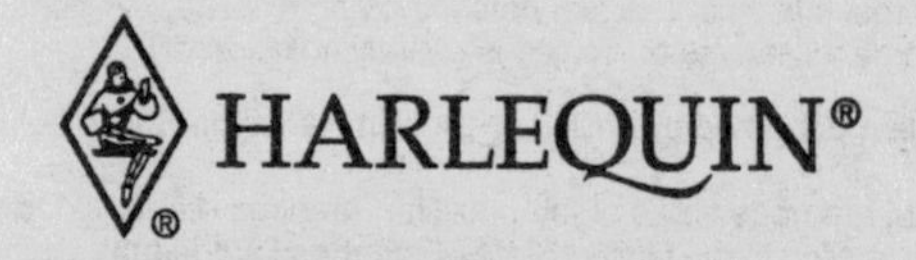

TORONTO • NEW YORK • LONDON
AMSTERDAM • PARIS • SYDNEY • HAMBURG
STOCKHOLM • ATHENS • TOKYO • MILAN • MADRID
PRAGUE • WARSAW • BUDAPEST • AUCKLAND

ISBN-13: 978-0-373-12753-5
ISBN-10: 0-373-12753-7

ONE NIGHT, ONE BABY

First North American Publication 2008.

This edition published by arrangement with Harlequin Books S.A.

www.eHarlequin.com

Printed in U.S.A.

All about the author...
Kate Hardy

KATE HARDY lives on the outskirts of Norwich, England, with her husband, two small children, a dog and too many books to count! She wrote her first book at age six, when her parents gave her a typewriter for her birthday. She had the first of a series of sexy romances published at twenty-five, and swapped a job in marketing communications for freelance health journalism when her son was born, so she could spend more time with him. She's wanted to write for Harlequin since she was twelve, and when she was pregnant with her daughter her husband pointed out that writing Harlequin Medical Romance™ books would be the perfect way to combine her interest in health issues with her love of good stories. Five years after selling her first Medical Romance novel, she branched out into writing for the Harlequin Presents series.

Kate is always delighted to hear from readers. Do drop in to her Web site at www.katehardy.com.

For Fi and Phil, godmothers extraordinaire,
with much love

CHAPTER ONE

PERFECT.

Absolutely *perfect*.

He was leaning against the stone pillar outside the office block, with his head tipped back slightly and his hands clasped just above his head, looking broodingly out onto the river Thames. His right knee was bent and his foot was flat against the wall. His dark, slightly curly hair looked as if he'd been running his fingers through it. And with that white shirt and dark suit trousers—no tie, no jacket, and the top button of his shirt undone—he looked tall, dark, handsome…and dangerous.

Exactly what Jane was looking for.

So why was she hanging back? Why wasn't she marching up to him and…?

'Because you're a wimp,' she told herself ruefully.

Charlie, her housemate, would've done it. Kissed him, then smiled and wished him a nice day before sauntering off. Then again, Charlie had *panache*. She could have got away with it. Jane knew she couldn't.

It was a daft idea anyway. Whoever walked up to a tall, dark, handsome man—a complete stranger—and kissed him?

All the same, he *was* gorgeous.

On impulse, she took her mobile phone from her bag; OK, so she wasn't brave enough to kiss him, but she'd take a photo.

Show her housemates the man who really fitted her fantasy—the one she wished she'd been brave enough to kiss. The camera zoom wasn't quite good enough, so she casually strolled closer. Close enough to get him right in the frame.

And just as she pressed the button to take the picture he glanced her way and saw what she was doing.

'Hey!'

Oh, no. Oh, no, no, no.

She backed away, but not fast enough, and the fingers of his right hand whipped down to encircle her wrist, hard as steel, trapping her where she stood. 'What's all this about?'

'Nothing.'

'You just took my photograph!'

This was so embarrassing. It would be good if the earth could open up and swallow her.

Preferably if time rewound first and she was swallowed up the very second before she'd taken that first step towards him. But, given that time travel wasn't possible, now would do very nicely.

He stared at her. He had the most beautiful greeny-grey eyes she'd ever seen, but right at that moment there wasn't a hint of softness or sweetness in them. 'Well?' he asked.

She shook her head. 'Look, I apologise.'

This was so *not* how it was meant to have happened.

'Would you mind letting me go, now?' She twisted her wrist in his grasp.

'Go…?' Then his gaze dropped to her wrist. 'You still haven't explained what that was all about.'

'I'm sorry. It was an impulse. A stupid impulse.' She switched the phone off and stuffed it back into her handbag. 'And right now I would very much like to go and hide behind that huge potted palm over there before anyone else stares at me,' she added, the last words uttered through gritted teeth.

To her surprise, he actually smiled.

It transformed his whole face. Turned him from the

Heathcliff type into someone much more accessible. She was glad he was still holding onto her wrist, because she didn't think her legs were going to hold her up for much longer. The tall, dark, handsome and brooding stranger had morphed into someone who was knee-bucklingly beautiful.

Not to mention way, way out of her league.

'I have a better idea,' he said. 'Coffee.'

'Coffee?' she repeated, nonplussed. Had she just missed something?

'I have a feeling that this is going to be a long story. And it'd be much more civilised to hear it over coffee.'

'But—' she frowned, puzzled '—weren't you taking a break from a meeting or something? At least, that's what it looked like.'

'It was an excruciatingly boring meeting.' He lifted one shoulder in the most elegant shrug she'd ever seen. 'My agent can deal with it for me.'

Agent? Was he famous, then? Or very important?

Of all the men outside all the buildings in all the world, she had to pick *this* one to photograph.

'Um—don't you need your jacket?'

'I wasn't wearing one in the first place.' He strode off, giving her no choice but to match her pace to his. 'But if it makes you feel better, I'll call Harry.'

'Harry?'

'My agent. Actually, you're right. It's only polite to let them know I'm not going back. Excuse me a moment.' He took a small, slim mobile phone from his pocket with his free hand and speed-dialled a number. 'Harry? Yes. No. Sorry.' He did at least sound genuinely contrite. 'Call you later, OK? Yes. Thanks.'

And by the time he'd slid the phone back into his pocket, they were in a café. Standing by the counter, ready to order.

'Espresso? Cappuccino?' he asked her.

'Skinny latte, please.'

'Make that two, please,' he said to the barista with a smile.

She coughed and looked pointedly at his fingers.

He inclined his head slightly and freed her wrist, paid for the coffees before she even had a chance to offer to buy them or at least pay her share, and then shepherded her over to a table overlooking the river.

'So. First things first. Your name?' he asked.

'Jane.'

'Jane what?'

'Redmond.'

He inclined his head in acknowledgement, but didn't extend his hand. 'Mitch Holland.'

Mitch. Short for Mitchell, perhaps? Though that wasn't a particularly English name, and his accent was most definitely English. Slightly on the posh side.

He took a sip of coffee and leaned back in his chair. 'So what was that all about?'

'I'm sorry. It was just…' She sighed. 'Thank you for the latte, Mr Holland.'

'Mitch,' he corrected. Then looked at her. Waiting for her answer.

Clearly he wasn't going to let her off. She'd have to explain. 'All right.' She turned the mug of coffee round and round in her hands. 'This is going to sound…' she blew out a breath '…ridiculous. Childish. *Stupid.*'

'Tell me anyway.'

'I'm twenty-five today.'

'Happy birthday. And?'

God, he was relentless. The type who'd never let anything go. 'I…' She squirmed. Even saying it made her feel whiny. Which just wasn't her. So she let the words go out in a rush. 'Nobody remembered. My parents, my brother, my housemates—even my colleagues at work.' Then she lifted her chin and stared him straight in the eye. Just so he knew she wasn't whinging. 'I'd already booked today as a holiday. Which left me with two choices: have a pity party and mope around the house, feeling sorry for myself, or spend the day doing things I've always wanted to do and never got round to doing. So I chose to enjoy my day.'

'Doing things you've always wanted to do.'

She could feel her skin heating. 'Things most women have done by the age of twenty-five.' And since she could guess what he was thinking, she threw the words at him. 'If you must know, top of the list was kissing a tall, dark, handsome stranger. But I was too chicken and took your photo instead.'

The corner of his mouth quirked. 'You were going to kiss me?'

She glared at him. Talk about maximum humiliation.

'Interesting.'

Before she realised his intentions, he'd pulled her onto his lap, slid one hand across the nape of her neck, and then his mouth was moving against hers. Teasing her. Tasting her. Tiny, nibbling kisses along her lower lip that incited her to open her mouth and let him deepen the kiss.

When she did, the tip of his tongue slid against hers. Probing softly, skilfully. Telling her he wanted her. Showing her how much she wanted him.

London faded. The noise in the café—people chattering, the clatter of cups against saucers, the thudding bass from someone's earphones—just vanished. No sound. No light, because her eyes were firmly closed. And her remaining senses were focused entirely on Mitch: the feel of his mouth against hers. The light, citrussy scent of whatever shower gel he'd used that morning. The taste of his mouth, coffee mingled with pure male.

It wasn't until the kiss ended that she realised his other hand was flat against her back, holding her close, and her own hands were tangled in his hair. Soft, sexy, rumpled hair.

Oh, hell.

She didn't *do* things like this.

She'd never, ever been kissed so thoroughly that she'd actually forgotten where she was.

And by a complete stranger, to boot.

'Happy birthday,' he said again, this time his tone much sweeter.

'Thank you. I think.' She levered herself off his lap and reclaimed her chair. And her dignity. Though she had a nasty feeling that her T-shirt was doing nothing to hide the erect state of her nipples.

'So that's what you're going to do today? Go around kissing strangers?'

There was definite amusement on his face now. Even though she knew he'd seen and it was too late, she folded her arms to hide her body's arousal. 'No. It was just one little thing on a list.' Empty bravado, and she'd just bet he knew it. After all, she'd already been stupid enough to tell him it was top of her list.

'So what else is on your list?'

She shrugged. 'A few things.' Things a man like Mitch Holland wouldn't be interested in.

Ten minutes ago, Mitch had had no idea that Jane Redmond even existed.

And now he'd kissed her. Properly. In public. Enough to be aroused.

Mad.

Really, he should just shut up. Drink his coffee, to be polite, and then say he needed to get back to his meeting.

Ha. Who was he trying to kid? He'd bought the coffee. He didn't have to be polite. He could walk out any time he chose.

The fact he didn't want to do that worried him.

The fact he wanted to know more about Jane Redmond worried him even more.

Relationships weren't even under the 'any other business' section of his agenda, let alone anywhere higher up. So why wasn't his mouth working on the same plans as the rest of his head? Why was it asking her, 'Such as?'

She frowned. 'Why do you want to know?'

His mouth was *really* on a roll. 'Seeing as I was involved with the first item.' A kiss. A kiss, he realised with shock, that he wanted to repeat. 'And things are often more fun when you do them with someone else.'

'Are you inviting yourself along?'

Absolutely not. No, no, and thrice no.

'Yes.'

She looked at him. 'No way would you do the things I want to do.'

This was his get-out. This was where he said, 'Yes, Jane, you're probably right. Have a nice birthday. Have a nice life,' and got the hell out of here.

But this was the first time in years he'd been challenged like this. The first time since, oh, he couldn't remember when, that he'd been intrigued by someone. And he wasn't ready to let that feeling go, just yet. So he said, 'Try me.'

She lifted her chin. 'All right. Paddling in the fountain in Trafalgar Square.'

'Sure. Though it means we'll have to evade the fountain monitors.'

She had one of those open faces that told you exactly what was going on in her head. Right now, that was pure puzzlement. Just to confirm it, she asked, 'What fountain monitors?'

'The people whose job it is to make sure nobody dips as much as a toe in the water. I think you're still allowed to smile, and possibly sit on the edge and have your photo taken. But no paddling.'

'Oh.' She was clearly aiming for cool and casual, but he could see the disappointment in her face. She flapped a dismissive hand. 'So that's another one crossed off, then.'

He shrugged. 'Not necessarily. I can keep a look out for the fountain monitors and distract them, if you're really set on it being Trafalgar Square. Or…' He really ought to shut up. But this was irresistible. The idea of spending a day doing things he wouldn't normally be doing. With a perfect stranger. Someone who didn't know him, wouldn't judge him. A day when he could maybe forget the past. Just *be.*

'Or?' she prompted.

'There's a fountain just a bit further up the South Bank from here. You can stand right in the middle with a wall of water going round you.'

She scoffed. '*You* wouldn't do that.'

Was she calling him stuffy? 'What makes you think that?'

'Your shirt's expensive. Not something you just picked up from a chain store.'

How did she know that?

'And if I look under the table,' she continued, 'I just bet I'll see a pair of handmade Italian shoes.'

'So?' he challenged.

'So you're not dressed for the things I want to do.'

'Hmm.' He looked at her. She was wearing a pastel-coloured T-shirt. Jeans? He hadn't really noticed her clothes when he'd dragged her off here—he'd been working purely on impulse. All he'd taken in were the facts that she had blue eyes, light brown hair cut in a short bob, was around six inches shorter than his own six feet, and she was very much the girl-next-door type.

The kind of woman he didn't want to get involved with.

The fact he'd just kissed her stupid in public was beside the point.

He took a quick look under the table. 'Linen trousers and loafers. Hmm. You're not planning on doing anything too messy, then.'

'I'm wearing comfortable clothes suitable for walking round the city on a warm April day,' she corrected.

He indicated his shirt. 'And who says this isn't comfortable?' Even if it was a handmade shirt. A decadent luxury that made being trapped in the city just about bearable.

It was her turn to look under the table. 'I was right about the shoes. You're not going to mess them up in a fountain.'

'Watch me,' he said, rising to the challenge. 'The fountain's first. What else?'

'Climbing to the top of St Paul's and whispering in the Whispering Gallery.'

This time he couldn't suppress the grin. 'How old were you when you made this list?'

'Not saying.'

'Fifteen,' he guessed.

Correctly, because her face turned the prettiest shade of pink. She blushed to the roots of her hair. And Mitch had to stop himself wondering if she blushed all over.

'I told you it was stupid,' she muttered, looking away.

'Actually,' he said, meaning it, 'it sounds like fun. You're on. What else?'

She stared at him. 'You're serious about this?'

'As serious as you are.'

'But y—'

'My time's my own,' he cut in gently, anticipating her objection.

'And you don't have a—well—a significant other who'd mind?'

'I don't have a significant other.' He had. Once. But—

No. He blocked the memories swiftly. 'And I'm not in the market for a relationship, either.' He needed to make that clear. And very much up front. This day had limits. A day of fun, yes. A day leading to another and another and a full-blown relationship, no. He was single and staying that way.

'I wasn't asking you for one,' she pointed out. 'And you're the one who's invited yourself along on my day.'

'Point taken.' He was pretty sure he already knew the

answer—Jane Redmond wasn't the sort to think about kissing a stranger if her heart was elsewhere—but he asked her anyway. 'I take it you don't have a significant other, either?'

'No.' Those blue eyes held a spark of defiance. 'And, just so you know, I'm not looking for one.'

Same as him. 'Good. We both know where we stand. Today's your birthday and we're going to have some fun.' And tomorrow was a different day. The beginning of the rest of their lives. When they'd never see each other again. 'So, what else is on this list?'

'Going on a boat on the Thames down to Greenwich, then walking up to the Observatory and standing on the meridian line. Climbing the Monument. Tea at the Ritz.' She wrinkled her nose. 'Except I think you have to book months in advance for that, and I haven't.'

Because clearly she hadn't expected to be spending her birthday on her own.

'We can always ask. Try and charm our way in.' He brushed a hand across his collar. 'I can pick up a tie some time before then. And if we can't have tea at the Ritz, we can go to Brown's or Fortnum's or the Savoy—make the best of it.'

She smiled. 'Thank you. Funny, I didn't think I'd end up spending my twenty-fifth birthday with a complete stranger.'

A birthday everyone seemed to have forgotten. And Jane, despite her girl-next-door looks, wasn't the kind of woman you forgot. There was something about her that had already imprinted itself on him—something he didn't want to analyse. This was meant to be about fun. 'Hey, a quarter of a century is something to celebrate.'

But there was something he needed to know. He deliberately made his voice more gentle. 'So how come your family forgot?'

She wrinkled her nose. 'They didn't *forget*, exactly.'

'I'm not with you.'

'Look, my parents are absolutely brilliant. They'll get an

OBE for services to archaeology one of these days and I'll be the one at the front clapping and cheering my head off.' She sighed. 'Except I'll also need to be the one to make sure they turn up on time and wear something a bit smarter than the stuff they wear on a dig.'

Just as Harry had to nag him to turn up on time and wear something that wasn't like his normal working clothes. He understood exactly where Jane's parents were coming from. 'So they just didn't realise that today's—well, today.'

He hadn't meant to sound judgemental, but she clearly took it that way, because she lifted her chin and glared at him. 'They're dedicated to their job and that's fine. I know they love me—I'm not insecure or neurotic. Mum and Dad just don't live in the real world.' She flapped her hand dismissively. 'They probably posted my birthday card yesterday and forgot that they're in Turkey right now and it takes a lot longer than a day for mail to get to London.'

Mmm. He'd been known to do that, too. 'What about your brother?'

'Alex is two years older than I am. Also an archaeologist. Like Mum and Dad, he's on a different planet and time zone from the rest of us.' She shrugged. 'As I said, it's not that they *deliberately* forgot. And when they realise, they'll be horribly upset that they missed it.'

Though Jane wouldn't be the one to remind them that they'd forgotten. Mitch knew that without having to ask. 'What about your friends? Your colleagues?'

He could virtually see the mask of bravery sliding onto her face. 'My housemates are all having a really hectic time at work. I'm not going to add to the stress by moaning that they forgot my birthday. And my colleagues are, um…'

'Archaeologists?' he asked, unable to resist teasing her.

'Archivists, actually.'

'Which is what? The desk version of archaeology?' he asked.

'Something like that,' she admitted. 'Instead of spending

your life digging in a muddy ditch, you spend your life looking for clues in old papers.'

Locked away from the world. Cocooned in the past. 'Sounds…' Safe and dull. Stuck in one place. *Entrapment.* 'Interesting.' It was the best word he could think of without insulting her.

She lifted her chin, clearly guessing his real thoughts. 'It is, actually. When you discover something that the world thought was lost for ever, or you make a connection that suddenly explains a lot of things.'

'So how come you're not an archaeologist, like the rest of your family?'

'When I was about fifteen, my parents did a summer dig at Vindolanda, one of the Roman forts on Hadrian's Wall. Because it was the holidays, Alex and I went with them. And then I found out about the letters at Vindolanda.' Her eyes lit up. The kind of passion he recognised: matching his feelings for his own job. 'It drew me so much more than patiently digging away in a trench: I loved trying to decipher the handwriting, crack the code—and finding out about the past from the documents. I knew then that was what I wanted to do.'

He could understand that; but what he couldn't understand was why she was so passionate about something so…safe. 'What's wrong with the present?' he asked.

'Nothing. I just happen to be interested in the past. So what do you do?' she asked.

Oh, she was going to love this. The complete opposite of herself. She clearly went to the same place day after day at work and lost herself in papers, whereas he was rarely in one place for very long. 'I chase storms,' he said mildly.

'You do *what*?' She stared at him as if he'd just grown a second head.

'I chase storms,' he repeated, and smiled at her. 'I take photographs of extreme weather.'

Her eyes widened. 'Tornadoes?'

'Sometimes.'

'In America?'

'Sometimes.' He couldn't resist bursting that particular bubble. 'Though, just for the record, the UK has more tornadoes per square mile than anywhere else in the world.'

'You're kidding.'

'On average there are thirty to forty a year. It's just that most of them are little and don't last long, and they tend to be in a rural or coastal area so you don't hear about them—the big ones that damage thousands of houses, like the ones in Birmingham and Kendal Rise, are pretty rare.'

'You chase storms.' She frowned. 'Is that what your meeting was about?'

'No. It was about an exhibition of my photographs.' He rolled his eyes. 'And I'd *much* rather be taking them than talking about them. I had to spend the whole of yesterday stuck inside, too. I loathe it. I'd rather be outside.'

She glanced up at the sky. 'Even though it doesn't look like stormy weather?'

'Even though,' he agreed. And the photographs were only half of his work. The showy half that supported the serious half. Not that Jane needed to know about that. 'I don't have a camera on me. I'm having a day off. And so, I think, are you.' He smiled and drained his coffee. 'Let's go find that fountain.'

CHAPTER TWO

MITCH couldn't remember enjoying a day so much. Going to the fountain on the South Bank and leaping over the gaps before the wall of water shot up between 'rooms'. Climbing the three hundred and eleven steps on the spiral staircase to the balcony at the top of the Monument—and then doing it all over again at St Paul's, where he whispered, 'Happy birthday,' from one side of the gallery and Jane whispered back, 'Thank you,' from the other side, their words perfectly amplified by the shape of the dome.

He brushed his mouth over hers when they reached the golden gallery at the highest point of the outer dome, two hundred and eighty feet above the ground. His head was spinning, and it was nothing to do with vertigo; it was everything to do with Jane.

From the way her pupils had grown huge, he could tell it was the same for her.

Instant attraction.

Crazy attraction.

He knew he wasn't her type—she'd go for someone who fossicked around in the past, not someone who wanted to leave it undisturbed. Someone who did safe, ordinary things—not someone who felt as if he were only alive when a storm whirled round him and whose work took him within five miles of a fast-moving tornado.

She wasn't his type, either. Not that he had a type, any more.

'Mitch?'

He pulled his thoughts together and forced himself to smile at her. 'It's just a birthday kiss,' he said lightly. Even though it felt like more than that. A hell of a lot more.

He was intensely aware of the woman beside him. The way the sun brought out little highlights of copper and gold in her light brown hair. The faint scent of jasmine. The fact his fingers were tingling with the desire to touch her.

Just as well they were in a public place.

But even so, after they'd made their way to the pier at Westminster and bought tickets for the river trip, he found himself sliding his right arm round her shoulders. Bringing her just that little bit closer to him on the seat. And she rested her left hand on his thigh for balance. A gesture more intimate than that of friends, let alone strangers. She was barely touching him, but it was as if he could feel every beat of blood through her veins. And he could definitely feel every beat of his own heart.

Just for today.

Just for today, she wasn't just 'Jane-Jane-Superbrain'. She wasn't the woman who organised her parents and her brother and her housemates. She wasn't the polite, quiet archivist who helped people find the documents they wanted and read ancient handwriting to unlock the secrets of the past.

Just for today, she was having fun. Doing things she'd always planned to do but never somehow seemed to find the time to fit them in. And she was doing them with the most gorgeous man she'd ever met. Walking up the hill to the Royal Observatory in Greenwich with her arm slung round his waist and his arm round her shoulders.

Like lovers.

She shivered.

They weren't lovers. And Mitch Holland most definitely

wasn't the man for her. He wasn't the type who'd settle down. He had the same wanderlust as her parents and her brother—probably even more so. At least archaeologists tended to stay in one place during a dig. Mitch, being a stormchaser, probably didn't even spend a week in the same place.

But today…today, it was good to be with him. The brooding stranger who'd turned out to have a sense of fun and be good company.

When they crossed the courtyard to the meridian line, he smiled at her. 'Standing on the meridian line, I think you said?'

'Astride it. With a foot in each hemisphere.' She smiled back. 'Which I know is an incredibly touristy thing to do.'

'Hey, it's *your* list. I'm not complaining.' He faced her, so that both of them were standing astride the narrow brass strip, then leaned over and lightly kissed her. 'Happy birthday—at longitude zero degrees, zero minutes and zero seconds.'

When they moved away from the line, he slid his arm round her shoulders again. 'Want to go into the museum?'

She shook her head. 'No time—not if we want to get back for tea at the Ritz. I know the Naval Museum pretty well, anyway.'

'You worked there?' he asked.

'Worked with them,' she corrected, 'on an exhibition about pirates.' At his surprised glance, she explained, 'I was involved on the documentary evidence side. Letters, journals, logbooks—that sort of thing.'

'So you're an expert on pirates.'

'A bit.'

His eyes glittered with amusement. 'The way you're looking at me—are you suggesting I'm a pirate?'

Jane laughed. 'When you're looking all brooding and fierce—like you were outside your meeting, earlier—yes.'

'Brooding and fierce? No-o-o. I'm a pussycat,' Mitch said.

'Right. And I'm the Queen of China.'

'China was ruled by emperors, not kings.'

'My point exactly,' she fenced back.

'I'm a *pussycat*,' Mitch insisted.

'You're a stormchaser.'

'What's to say I can't be both?'

Everything. Mitch was most definitely more pirate than pussycat. She smiled. 'Let's have lunch.'

'What do you have in mind?'

'A sandwich in the park?' she suggested. 'I'm buying.'

'No, you're not. It's your birthday, so *I'm* buying. And don't argue.' The crinkles at the corners of his eyes took the bossiness from his words.

A few minutes later, they were sitting on the hill with sandwiches and bottles of chilled water, enjoying the view over London. When they'd finished eating, Mitch stretched out on the grass and stared up at the sky. 'Nothing beats the colour of the sky on an English spring day.'

Jane tipped her head back to look up, and he pulled her down so her head was pillowed on his shoulder.

'And those,' he said, 'are my favourite clouds. Cirrus.' He pointed out the delicate white streaks above them.

'They look as if they've been brushed on the sky by a feather,' Jane said.

'They're formed by ice crystals high up in the atmosphere,' he explained. 'That's what makes them look so feathery.'

She smiled. 'I bet you're as nerdy about cloud formations as I am about palaeography.'

'Probably,' he admitted, laughing. 'Harry's eyes glaze over when I start going on about the different types of clouds.'

'Do you take pictures of clouds like these as well as storms?'

'Yes. I've always been fascinated by them.'

She nestled closer. 'So what made you become a stormchaser?'

She felt him tense for a moment. 'I suppose it was a natural progression from meteorology.'

It didn't feel as if that was the whole explanation, but she didn't want to spoil the day by pushing him. 'Are you telling me you used to be a weatherman—one of these people who tell us it's going to be fine and then it rains all day?'

He laughed. 'No. I didn't do TV or radio forecasts. I worked on models of climate systems. Analysing cloud formations, measuring atmospheric pressure—that sort of thing. Basically, how storms start and how we can predict their movements.' He paused. 'I was in Antarctica for a while. It's an incredible place.'

Lonely. Bleak. Isolated—even more so than the sites where her parents and her brother worked. How could he bear it? She was cocooned in the archives for most of the time, but there were always people around her. People who needed her to help show them how to find something, how to interpret it. 'Uh-huh,' she said carefully. 'And there's also no sunshine for the whole of winter.'

'If you're working on documents, I bet you don't even notice what the weather's like outside,' he countered.

'I do when I go for a walk at lunchtime.'

He laughed. 'I guess going for a walk in Antarctica's a bit different.'

'You're talking sub-zero temperatures, aren't you?' She grimaced.

He shifted so that he was leaning on his side. 'Are you cold?'

'No.'

'Hmm.' He rested the back of his hand against her cheek, as if testing her temperature. It was the lightest possible contact, but it made every nerve-end flicker to life. Wanting more.

'Better safe than sorry,' he said, and dipped his head. Moved his mouth against hers—the lightest, sweetest touch.

And it was like a flame to touchpaper.

Jane wasn't sure when or how he'd moved, but then Mitch was practically lying on top of her. His knees had nudged hers apart and he was supporting his weight on his knees and his elbows; but she was very aware of the hardness of his chest against her breasts, the flatness of his abdomen against her own softer belly.

Her hands stroked down his back, feeling the play of his muscles. Gorgeous. Broad shoulders, narrow waist, and the most perfect bottom. He'd be lethal in a pair of tight, faded jeans.

And, God, his mouth. Teasing and promising and demanding, all at once. So even though her head was yelling that they were in a public place, that kissing each other like this really wasn't a good idea, her body wasn't listening. It was enjoying the sensation of Mitch's body pressed against hers, of his tongue against hers, sliding into her mouth the way she wanted his body to slide into hers. The ultimate closeness.

When he broke the kiss, they stared at each other. His eyes were as hot and stormy as the weather he chased: no softness there, just pure passion. There was a slash of colour across his cheekbones. His mouth looked reddened and slightly swollen—and she'd guess that hers was in pretty much the same state. She'd matched him nibble for nibble, bite for bite. And she could feel his erection pressing against her, just as she was sure he could feel the hardness of her nipples. Aroused. Aching. *Wanting.*

'Definitely a pirate,' she whispered.

'Which, unless I'm mixing my metaphors, makes you a siren.' He bent his head again and caught her lower lip gently between his.

Desire rippled down her spine. 'Mitch. *Mitch.* This isn't supposed to be happening.'

'No.' He levered himself off her and rolled over onto his back. 'I'm sorry.'

'Me, too.' Though she wasn't quite sure what she was more sorry about the fact that she'd just lost control in a public place, not caring how abandoned her behaviour was, or the fact that he'd stopped kissing her.

'I take it that wasn't on your list.'

She coughed. 'Er—no.'

'We both know where we stand. Today's just today. And it's unfair of me to pressure you. Especially as…' His voice faded. 'We'd better start heading back if we want to go and have tea at the Ritz.' He stood up, then leaned down to take her hand and pull her to her feet. 'Come on. I need to find a tie. I'm pretty sure they insist on one.'

They did. And a jacket—he managed to borrow one. But even though Mitch was clearly being charming, the *maître d'* wasn't able to help. 'There's no room for us to have a proper tea—you're right, you have to book up,' he told Jane when he returned. 'But we can sit on one of the sofas over there and have a cup of tea, if you like.' He shrugged. 'Up to you—if you want the full works with cucumber sandwiches and scones with jam and cream, we can go somewhere else.'

'A cup of tea at the Ritz would be just fine, thanks,' she said with a smile.

It was just how she'd imagined it: a waiter with white gloves, bearing a proper silver teapot and a silver strainer, poured tea into delicate china cups. There was a man playing Schumann on a grand piano. And it was the best cup of tea she'd ever tasted. All the sweeter, because she paid the bill on her way back from the powder room—which meant Mitch couldn't protest without drawing attention to himself.

When they left, once Mitch had returned the jacket, the doorman offered to call them a taxi.

'Thanks,' Mitch said, 'but there's no need. We're walking.'

And this was it. The end of her day. Jane summoned a smile as they stepped outside. 'I can't remember the last time I enjoyed myself so much. Thanks for making my birthday special.'

'My pleasure. I enjoyed it, too,' he said. 'But your birthday's not over yet. How about having dinner with me?' He tipped his head slightly to one side. 'But where I have in mind, you'll need a dress and proper shoes.'

She frowned. 'What?'

'You look fine as you are,' he added hastily, 'but the place I'm thinking of prefers you to, um, dress up a bit.'

She grinned. 'Not in stormchaser gear, then.'

He grinned back. 'Don't believe everything you see in the movies. Though I admit, I'll have to change as well—wear a jacket. Not a borrowed one, this time.'

'I'll go home and change and meet you later, then?'

'I've got a better idea,' he said. 'Let's go shopping.'

'What? Why?'

'To get you a dress and some shoes.'

She shook her head. 'There's really no need.'

'Humour me,' he said softly. The sexy, stormy look was back in his eyes. 'If you're worried about money, don't be—I'm not exactly poor and there are more important things than money anyway.'

She'd agree with that. Definitely.

'Today's your birthday. You bought me tea at the Ritz, so I'd like to buy you dinner. And because I don't live in London, I'll be at a loose end tonight if you turn me down. All on my lonesome,' he added, giving her a little-boy-lost look that she just knew was manufactured.

'That,' she said, 'is emotional blackmail.'

'No. I've enjoyed your company. I'd like to have dinner with you,' he said simply. 'And we said today was just for one day. There's still quite a while left until tomorrow.'

Put that way, what could she say except yes?

Half an hour later, they were in Oxford Street—she'd refused his suggestion of a boutique in South Kensington, because she really didn't go to the kind of place where you had to wear haute couture. She preferred to go to the kind of shop that sold stylish, well-made and comfortable clothes that didn't require a second mortgage—and where she could pick up just about anything and know that it'd fit her without having to try it on. And the same was true for underwear.

'You hate shopping, don't you?' Mitch asked.

'What makes you say that?'

'Because every other female I know would jump at the chance to go clothes-shopping, and browse in a dozen shops before even trying anything on. My sister is a nightmare. She tries everything on—and then drags you round the complete set of shops again because she can't make up her mind what she wants.'

'Some women enjoy doing that.' Jane shrugged. 'I can think of better ways of spending my time.'

'Mmm-hmm.'

She met his gaze and saw the sensual flare in those beautiful grey-green eyes. The promise.

Oh, no. That hadn't been what she'd meant. She'd rather be pottering about in the archives or reading a good book on the riverbank or sitting in the kitchen eating cake and chatting to her housemates than shopping for clothes. She really hadn't been thinking about sex.

But it was written in his eyes.

And now he'd put the thought into her head, her mouth went dry. 'I…'

'Later,' he said softly. He hailed a taxi, which took them to a very swish block of flats in the West End. Mitch swiped a card-key through the slot next to the front door, and when a green light flashed on the panel he pushed the door open and ushered her through.

'I thought you said you didn't live in London?' she asked as he opened his front door.

'I don't live anywhere. Except maybe out of my suitcase,' he conceded.

She frowned as she stepped inside the small studio flat. 'Then what's this place?'

'A short let. Harry arranged it.' He shrugged. 'It's marginally better than staying in a hotel. I see enough hotels and the like in storm season.'

It was a single living room with a sofa bed, a table, some cupboards and a tiny kitchen. She supposed this would give him more flexibility, so he could make himself a snack whenever he chose and didn't have to worry about disturbing other guests, but it still didn't feel like home. The room looked bare. There was no clutter on the surfaces apart from a single bowl of fruit, no personal touches. And she'd just bet that nearly all of the cupboards and drawers were empty. There was nothing here at all to give any clue to who Mitch was, at heart.

Her thoughts must have shown on her face because he rolled his eyes. 'Look, doing what I do, I'm used to living out of a suitcase. I travel with the weather system. So it really doesn't bother me. I don't need roots.'

Didn't he? Everyone needed roots.

What had been so bad in Mitch's life that nowadays he preferred not to stay in one place too long?

Not that she was going to ask him. She knew he'd change the subject. Whatever it was, she had a feeling it was linked to the shadows in his eyes. The shadows she'd seen when his fingers had encircled her wrist and he'd demanded to know what that kiss was all about.

'Do you want me to make you a coffee while you have a shower and change?' he asked.

'Thanks.' She was glad of his suddenly brisk, businesslike manner. Because she couldn't stop thinking about that look in his eyes. The way he'd kissed her. And the fact that there was a sofa bed very, very close to them.

'There's a hairdryer around somewhere if you need it—I'll dig it out for you—and a bathrobe behind the door. Help yourself to shampoo and what have you.'

She wasn't sure whether she was more relieved or disappointed that he hadn't suggested sharing the shower with her. Though, since that kiss on the hill in Greenwich, he'd kept his hands and his mouth to himself. Again, she felt that odd mixture of disappointment and relief.

'You must be temporarily deranged,' she told herself. Mitch Holland was a complete stranger. Yes, she'd enjoyed his company on her impromptu day, but she knew next to nothing about him. Just that he was a stormchaser who was soon going to have an exhibition of his photographs somewhere in London.

It was nowhere near enough information.

She'd been stupid enough to let him pay for her dress.

And now she was in his flat.

Next to naked.

Would he expect payment in kind?

She pulled the belt a little bit tighter, wrapped her wet hair in a towel and walked out of the bathroom.

Mitch was sitting on the sofa with a mug of coffee in his left hand and a laptop balanced on his knee; he was tapping keys and frowning at the screen. He looked up when she entered the room. 'That was quick.'

She tried for lightness. 'Want to check I washed behind my ears?'

He laughed. 'You're about twenty years too old for that.' He placed the mug and the laptop on the table, then walked over to the little galley kitchen and switched the kettle on again.

The way he walked made her think of a pirate. That, the white shirt—again with no tie, because he'd taken it off the minute they'd left the Ritz—and the fact he had the beginnings of stubble made her want to unbelt the robe and let it fall to the floor.

What the hell was wrong with her? She'd been acting out of character all day. She was a quiet, sensible archivist. Not the kind of woman who went to a strange man's flat at the drop of a hat. Not the kind of woman who threw herself at an attractive man she barely knew.

When Mitch handed her the mug of coffee, his fingers

brushed against hers. To her horror, her hand actually shook and she spilled the coffee.

'Sorry,' she muttered.

'No problem.' He hunted in the cupboard under the sink, retrieved some paper towelling and mopped up the spill. 'So why are you suddenly nervous?'

'I…'

'Jane. Dinner means *dinner*, not that I expect you to pay me with sex.' The corner of his mouth quirked. 'Unless you want to, of course.'

She stopped breathing.

'The hairdryer's on the table. Now, I'm going to have a shower. I'll dress in the bathroom.' He took a suit and shirt on a hanger from the front of a cupboard. 'Knock on the door when it's OK for me to come back in.'

Not a pirate after all, then. A gentleman. One who'd wait for her to dry her hair and get dressed. No pressure.

'Thank you,' she said quietly.

He paused in the bathroom doorway. 'Did you *really* think I was going to offer to show you my etchings?'

The teasing glint in his eyes made her realise he was trying to make her feel at ease. 'Hey. I thought you were a photographer, not an engraver.'

He laughed. 'Of course, you're an archivist—you'd know about that sort of thing. See you in a bit.' Just before he closed the door, he added, 'I've ordered a taxi for half an hour's time. Does that give you long enough?'

'Not all women spend hours getting ready, you know.'

He winked. 'Bet you I'm ready before you are.'

She winked back. 'Bet you you're not.'

'I'll be thinking of your loser's forfeit,' he said, and closed the door.

Traditionally, the loser of a bet between a man and a woman would pay in kisses.

But Mitch had said he wasn't expecting sex.

Unless you want to.

The words echoed in her head. He'd been teasing—at least, she *thought* he had—but she'd seen that hot, smoky look in his eyes. A look that meant it was a serious offer. And he was leaving the choice to her.

Every nerve-end tingled. What would it be like to make love with Mitch Holland? If just a kiss could send her weak at the knees, she'd probably pass out when his body slid into hers.

She dragged in a breath, realising she'd just thought 'when', not 'if'.

Trying not to think about having sex with Mitch occupied her all the way through drying her hair—using the little compact mirror from her handbag, as there didn't seem to be another one in the flat—then putting on her dress, adding lipstick and mascara and putting her discarded clothes and shoes neatly in the carrier bag that had held her dress.

Then she remembered the bet.

No way was she ready to lose this.

She rapped on the bathroom door. 'Ready when you are.'

'I'm ready now,' Mitch said, and opened the door.

She scoffed. 'No way. You're still knotting your tie.' She was about to tell him that she'd won—but her mouth felt as if it were full of sand as he shrugged on his suit jacket. He'd looked good enough to eat when he'd borrowed that jacket at the Ritz. But this one was made to measure: a very dark grey, teamed with another of the handmade white shirts and an understated silk tie. And he looked truly gorgeous. A pirate with a veneer of civilisation, admittedly—but still a pirate.

She couldn't help lifting one hand and touching his face. Freshly shaven: soft, smooth and so very sexy. Her fingertips tingled at the contact; she could tell it affected him the same way, because his eyes went sultry. He took her hand and kissed the pads of her fingertips, just where her skin had been against his.

Her breath hitched. 'Mitch.'

'So what's my loser's forfeit?' he asked, his voice low and husky and daring her to tell him to take her to bed.

She swallowed hard. 'I…' Right at that moment, she couldn't think straight enough to answer. 'Later.'

'You look fantastic in that dress, by the way.' He nibbled his way down to her palm. Dropped a kiss in the middle. Touched the tip of his tongue to the pulse beating crazily in her wrist.

If he reached behind her now and undid the zip of her dress, she wouldn't stop him. She'd just step out of the puddle of material. And she'd start undressing him, too. Unbutton his shirt. Slide her hands against his washboard-flat stomach. Unbutton—

A horn beeped, and he took a step backwards. 'Our taxi.'

'Uh-huh.'

'Leave your things here,' he said. 'We'll collect them after dinner.'

Dinner? He could think about food, when his mouth had just been gliding against her skin and sending her mind way out of control?

But she followed him out of the flat and into the taxi.

The restaurant was in a little back street. To reach it, they had to go through a tiny little courtyard into a potager garden, then through the kitchen itself, where the *maître d'* met them: a man dressed in mid-eighteenth-century clothing, including a braided frock coat, breeches, and a curled and powdered wig. Jane had to try very hard not to stare.

'I had no idea this place even existed,' she whispered when the *maître d'* had greeted them and was leading them through to their table.

'A select few know about it,' Mitch said. 'My father brought me here the day after I graduated.'

So this place was special to him? The fact he was bringing her here said a lot.

Her eyes widened as they walked into the restaurant. She should've expected it, given the *maître d'*s costume, but it still surprised her. It was like stepping back into the eighteenth century: all gilt and florid decoration around the picture frames and mirrors that crammed the walls, a deep red silk ceiling that billowed like the inside of a sultan's harem, and starched white damask tablecloths that she'd guess covered highly polished wood underneath. All the cutlery was solid silver, as was the very ornate candelabrum, and the knives had bone handles.

And there was no menu.

The question must have shown in her face, because he smiled. 'Trust me, the food is incredible.'

'You don't get a choice?' she whispered when the *maître d'* left them.

'Wait and see.'

The *maître d'* returned with two glasses of champagne—very thin smoked glass, where the stem was actually part of the champagne flute and the bubbles rose gently from the very base of the glass.

'Happy birthday,' he said softly, raising his glass.

'Thank you.' And it was turning out to be way more special than she'd imagined.

The *maître d'* brought them some canapés. 'Now, tonight the chef has decided to offer…' He reeled off three choices of hors d'oeuvres and three main courses. 'Served with a *mélange* of vegetables, of course.'

The food was as incredible as Mitch had told her. And when it came to puddings… 'I can't choose between the lemon polenta cake and the chocolate cheesecake,' she said.

'Simple. Let's order them both and share them.'

'Is that allowed?' she whispered.

He smiled. 'I should think so.'

When their puddings arrived, she realised he hadn't meant

just eating half and swapping plates. Because he held out a spoonful of lemon polenta cake and encouraged her to lean forward to taste it.

Oh, God.

'My turn,' he said softly.

Her gaze was focused on his mouth as she held out a spoonful of the incredibly rich and chocolaty pudding. Had the same thoughts been running through his head when he'd fed her the lemon pudding? Had he wanted to lean forward and brush his mouth against hers, the way she wanted to kiss him?

'Delectable,' he said.

And she didn't think he was talking about the pudding; when she'd leaned forward, she'd given him a prime view of her cleavage. And she'd seen his eyes darken. Seen the same desire there that was flooding through her right now.

Pudding was followed by incredibly strong but good coffee and petits fours. And then Mitch called another taxi. 'We need to collect your stuff from mine,' he told her as he held the passenger door open for her.

'Of course.' So this was it. Goodbye in the making. 'Thank you for today. It's been fabulous,' she said, meaning it. She leaned forward, intending to kiss his cheek—but he moved and she ended up with her mouth against his. A touch that made her lips tingle. Particularly when he slid his arm round her and pulled her onto his lap, leaning back against the seat so that she had to hold onto him for balance.

She kissed him all the way back to his flat. Long and deep and hard, not caring that the taxi driver could see in the rear-view mirror. The desire running through her was much, much headier than the bubbles from the bottle of champagne they'd shared.

Finally, the taxi pulled up outside the flat. She followed Mitch inside.

This was it.

Goodbye.

She picked up the carrier bag with the clothes she'd worn earlier.

'Thanks for everything,' she said.

What did she say now? Have a nice life? Goodbye, stranger?

A stranger whose lips were reddened and slightly swollen with kisses. *Her* kisses. And her mouth probably looked equally well kissed.

'Jane,' he said softly. 'There weren't any strings to today. I'm not looking for a relationship. Neither are you.'

Which was when she realised she'd thought things had changed. That what had happened between them on the hill at Greenwich had changed everything.

Clearly it hadn't.

Disappointment plummeted in her stomach.

'I'm not expecting you to make love with me.'

Which was a good thing—wasn't it?

'But,' he added huskily, 'if you choose to stay with me tonight, I'd…' He blew out a breath and removed his tie. 'Ah, hell. I'm just about hanging onto my last shreds of self-control. I want to take that dress off you, Jane. Right here, right now.'

He'd made it clear that this was just about here and now. Not the future. Tomorrow was another day—the first day of the rest of their lives, when they'd never see each other again.

She should be sensible and refuse.

But it wasn't every day you were twenty-five.

It wasn't every day you had the chance to spend just one night with a man who took your breath away. Pure pleasure, with no consequences.

She smiled, took a step forward and undid the top button of his shirt.

CHAPTER THREE

MITCH went absolutely still, so Jane undid the next button. And the next. And then she untucked his shirt from his trousers and undid all the rest of the buttons.

He looked amazing. Bare-chested, slightly dishevelled—she'd really messed up his hair when she'd kissed him in the taxi—and mouth-wateringly sexy. She wanted to touch him. And then touch him some more.

He shrugged off his jacket; she splayed her hands against his bare chest, then slid them down his washboard-flat abdomen. His musculature was perfect; he felt as good as he looked. 'This isn't from working out in a gym, is it?' she asked, stroking his pectorals.

There was a slight edge to his smile. 'What do you think?'

'I can't see you as a gym gorilla.'

'I need to be fit for my work. I run, most days.'

She traced his collar-bones with her middle finger. 'Do you know how hot you look, in that prissy white shirt?' she whispered.

'Prissy?' He raised an eyebrow. 'You're calling me *prissy*?'

'Yup.' She touched the tip of her tongue to the hollow of his collar-bones. 'And hot.'

He sucked in a breath. 'Is that why you took my photograph on the South Bank, this morning?'

She nodded. 'It had to be a tall, dark, handsome stranger.

And even though you looked in a seriously bad mood, you were irresistible.'

'I'm glad to hear it.' He dipped his head and brushed his mouth against hers. 'So are you undressing me, or what?'

She nodded. 'I'm just taking my time about it. Enjoying the view.'

He smiled. 'Would this be the champagne talking?'

'Partly,' she admitted. 'But I know exactly what I'm doing. And I have no regrets whatsoever.'

He stole a kiss. 'No regrets. Sounds good to me. It's a deal.'

She slipped her hands inside his shirt and drew her palms down his sides, touching warm, soft, smooth skin. 'You feel beautiful.'

'That's not fair. I haven't touched you yet.' He coughed. 'You're wearing too much.'

She pursed her lips and wiggled her hips. 'What are you going to do about it, then, storm boy?'

'What I wanted to do when I saw you in that dress for the first time, tonight.' His gaze held hers as he reached out, unzipped her dress, then pushed the material from her shoulders and let it slide to the floor in a puddle. 'Mmm. Gorgeous.' He traced her collar-bones, echoing the way she'd touched him. And then he raised the stakes by drawing one finger slowly down her sternum to the vee between her breasts, making her shiver.

She wanted to step forward and jam her mouth to his. But there was something she had to deal with, first. 'These are going to crease. As I said, no regrets. And I would hate to spoil these.' She stepped out of her dress and picked it up, together with his jacket, then hung his jacket over the back of a dining chair, shook the folds out of her dress and laid it neatly on top of his jacket.

Mitch chuckled.

'What's so funny?' She frowned at him. Was he laughing at her?

'I should've guessed that would bother you, leaving clothes on the floor.'

'So you're telling me you're a slob?'

He lifted one shoulder in an elegant half-shrug. 'I told you, I live out of a suitcase. My clothes don't usually see an iron.'

'Your shirt was ironed today.'

'Laundry service,' he told her with a grin. 'Harry's attempt to civilise me enough for a meeting. That's where you and I are poles apart: I'm used to chaos, and you're used to absolute order.'

Well, of course. Given the millions of documents where she worked, if things weren't exactly in their place you'd never be able to retrieve them. She'd learned to be meticulous about keeping things in the right place, putting things away before they were damaged or lost. And yet his work involved tornadoes, the ultimate in disorder. How opposite could you get? '"East is East and West is West?"' she quoted.

He gave her the sexiest, most predatory smile she'd ever seen. 'Ah, but I'm looking forward to the twain meeting.'

The fact he knew the quotation and could cap it made a shiver of desire run through her. He had a gorgeous voice. What she'd give to hear him reading poetry. Donne, Marvell—Catullus. And then acting out the poet's suggestions…

She dragged in a breath. 'We might have a problem there. Because you're wearing a lot more than I am.'

'So what are you going to do about it?' He tipped his head on one side. 'I'm a man of action. You're a woman of words.'

'Challenge accepted,' she said, and slid the shirt from his shoulders.

He was just perfect. He had an athlete's physique: broad shoulders, a narrow waist, defined upper arms. There was a light sprinkling of hair on his chest—not so much to be off-putting, but not boyish either.

There was nothing boyish at all about Mitch Holland.

He was six feet of pure man.

'Hmm. So I'm bare-chested.' He traced a finger along the lacy edge of her bra. 'You, on the other hand, are not.'

'Ah, but I'm not wearing my dress. And you're still wearing trousers.'

He gave her a broad, inviting smile.

So he thought she'd chicken out, did he? And he'd called her a woman of words. His opposite. Well, she'd show him that she could be a woman of action. She reached out. Unbuckled his belt. Undid the button at his waistband. Took the tab of his zip between fingers she willed not to shake, and slowly drew it down. She could feel his erection pressing against her as she pulled the zip downwards; there was absolutely no way he could deny that he was turned on. She had physical proof that he was as aroused as she was.

She pushed the material downwards so his trousers fell over his hips and pooled around his ankles. He kicked off his shoes and stepped out of his trousers—and she noted that he removed his socks at the same time.

Her thoughts must have shown on her face, because there was a twinkle in his eye when he said, 'Socks aren't sexy.'

No, but those soft black jersey jockey shorts were. *Incredibly* sexy. She breathed in deeply. 'Tights aren't sexy, either.'

'Then allow me to help you.' He hooked his fingers into the waistband of her half-slip and her tights, and slid them both down together.

Oh, lord. She'd never been undressed like this before. Slowly. By a man with eyes that were hungry for just her.

He stroked her buttocks and thighs as he uncovered her skin, then dropped to his knees before her. He made her lift one foot so he could remove her shoe and then peel her tights off; he caressed her instep as he bared it, then did the same with her other foot.

It was enough to make her knees go weak. A man who found an erogenous zone she hadn't even known existed.

He rocked back slightly and looked up at her. 'What a view,' he said, his voice husky. He brushed her inner thigh with his mouth. 'I want you, Jane. More than I've wanted anyone in a long, long time.'

The words thrilled her. So it was the same for him. This urgent need. Wanting to touch and stroke and taste until the desire bubbled over and exploded. 'That makes two of us,' she admitted.

Tonight was just tonight. No consequences. So there was something they needed to do, first. 'Condoms? You have some?' If not, she was pretty sure she did. Somewhere in her bag. At least, she hoped she had. If they had to call a halt now, the frustration would drive her insane.

'Don't worry,' he said softly. 'I'll take care of you.'

'Just for tonight.'

'Just for tonight,' he confirmed. He rose to his feet and linked his fingers through hers. 'Come to bed, Jane. Make love with me.'

'Bed?' She stared at the sofa.

'Ah, yes.' He rolled his eyes. 'One time when a hotel room might have been more useful. Hold that thought a moment.'

Deftly, he turned the sofa into a bed, then opened a cupboard and took out the duvet and pillows. When he'd finished making the bed, he sat on the edge and held out his hand.

Silently, she went over to him. He pulled her onto his lap. 'I've wanted to do this ever since this morning,' he said, his voice soft and husky with desire.

'Since you kissed me in the café?'

'Uh-huh.' He brushed his mouth against hers. 'And I want to kiss you now,' he whispered. 'Properly.' He cupped her face and caught her lower lip between his. She opened her mouth, letting him deepen the kiss. He slid the tip of his tongue against hers, teasing and demanding at the same time.

When her fingers tangled in his hair, he moved his hands. Slid them down her neck, stroking and soothing and promising. Then over her shoulders, pushing the straps of her bra down as she moved. He was still kissing her when one hand trailed its way between her shoulder blades and deftly unclasped her bra; finally, he let her breasts spill into his hands, taking their weight and cupping them, his thumbs rubbing against her nipples.

She shivered, and he broke the kiss.

'You feel amazing,' he said softly.

And then he looked.

His breath hissed. 'You're beautiful. Perfect,' he said.

She wasn't sure which of them moved, but then she was straddling him. She could feel the hardness of his erection pressing against her, just as it had when he'd kissed her on the hillside at Greenwich.

Mitch kissed her mouth again, then traced a path across to her ear, down the sensitive cord at the side of her neck, and then finally, finally took one nipple into his mouth and sucked. She gasped and slid her fingers into his hair, the pressure of her fingertips urging him on. When he switched sides and paid attention to her other breast, she was rocking against him, needing more, getting nearer and nearer to the edge.

He slid one finger under the edge of her knickers and drew a fingertip along the length of her sex. When he touched her clitoris, she shivered.

'You like that?' he murmured against her ear, his breath fanning her skin.

Right at that moment, when he was circling her with clever fingers that seemed to know exactly how and where she liked being touched, she wasn't capable of speaking proper words. 'Mmm.'

'Good.' He continued stroking her, lightly enough to tease her and yet firmly enough to make her desire rise higher and higher and higher. He nuzzled between her breasts, then slowly kissed his way upwards.

Breathing was difficult. Seriously difficult. Every sensation in her body seemed to be concentrated around his hand and his mouth. She tipped her head back, offering him her throat; when he traced a necklace of kisses across it, she quivered against his hand. So close, so very close…

And then he stopped.

She dragged her eyelids open and stared at him. It felt as if she were suspended in space, as if she'd been spinning in a whirlwind and suddenly everything had stopped, gone calm. The eye of the storm.

'What's wrong?'

He smiled. 'Nothing. I'm just not ready for you to come, yet.'

'I… That's not fair, Mitch.'

'Storms are more spectacular,' he said, 'when they build slowly. When the pressure changes and the air starts to spin, warm chasing cold. Then it picks up speed. Gets more intense. And then, when the storm hits…' his eyes glittered '…everything shatters.'

'And that's what you're planning to do to me?'

He leaned forward and brushed his mouth against hers. '*With* you. Because I'm going to be there too, all the way.' He gently moved her off his lap onto the bed, then stripped off his shorts, stood up and walked over to a cupboard.

She watched him, mesmerised. The way he walked… Naked, he was beautiful. The perfect rear view. Enough to make her wish she could paint.

He rummaged in the cupboard, and she watched the play of muscles across his back.

And then he turned to face her, and she forgot to breathe.

She'd never seen a man she'd wanted more.

And tonight, he was all hers.

Tonight.

Because right now he had a handful of condoms. Condoms he hadn't bought when they'd gone shopping earlier. So he'd been prepared for something to happen. Did he always have them on him, just in case, as she did? Or because he was never in one place long: did he do this everywhere? Find a woman who took his fancy and spend the night with her?

As if he'd guessed her thoughts, he said softly, 'It's not a case of a new town, a new girl. I'm picky.' A corner of his mouth lifted. 'And I could point out that I'm not the one who started all this.'

'All I did was take a photograph,' she defended herself. 'I wasn't the one who introduced kissing into the equation.'

'Because you were too chicken.' The challenge in his eyes made something tighten deep in her belly. 'Are you too chicken now?'

She lifted her chin. 'No.'

'Then do it,' he said, stretching out on the bed beside her and propping himself up on one elbow. 'Kiss me.'

She reached up to him and did as he said. Slid her tongue against his lower lip and teased him into opening his mouth beneath hers. Let her hand drift down over his ribcage, across his side, over the curve of his buttocks.

'You're beautiful,' she said softly as she broke the kiss.

'So are you,' he said. 'Perfect curves. A real woman, not a stick insect.' He stroked the curve of her hip, cupped one breast. 'And no, that isn't an oblique way of calling you fat. You're soft and feminine and you turn me on. Big time. I want to touch you. Kiss you all over. Taste you until you're quivering and your head is spinning.'

'I thought,' she said, 'I was supposed to be the one of words and you were the one of action?'

He laughed. 'Since you mention it…' He dipped his head. Kissed the hollows of her throat, caressed her skin until she was near to purring. And then he removed her knickers, the last barrier between them.

'Just you and me,' he whispered, and stroked his way up the inside of her thighs. Touched her with his clever fingertips until she was quivering.

When he replaced his hands with his mouth, he fulfilled the promise he'd made. Her head was spinning. And just when she thought she'd reached the edge, he stopped. Leaving her dangling. One tiny touch would do it.

And he obviously knew that and intended to drive her crazy.

She dragged in a breath. 'I think I hate you.'

'No, you don't.'

She opened her eyes and stared at him. 'I do.'

He grinned. 'I promise you, you won't.'

He ripped open the foil packet and rolled the condom onto his erect penis. Then he knelt between her thighs. 'Now?' he asked softly.

'Now,' she agreed.

When his body eased into hers, she stopped thinking.

Just felt.

Pressure rising, rising, rising with every thrust. Not that he settled into a rhythm—just when she thought he was taking it slowly, he pushed hard and fast, sending her near to spiralling over the edge. And then he calmed everything down again. Slow and easy. Keeping her right on the brink.

'I'm going crazy, here,' she whispered.

'Good.' He caught her lower lip between his, then slid his tongue into her mouth, mirroring the thrust of his body inside hers.

All she could do was wrap her legs round his waist and hold on.

Every nerve-end in her body felt incredibly sensitised. She could feel every hair on his chest brushing against her skin. Her nipples were so hard, they almost hurt. And her temperature was definitely rising to fever pitch.

And beyond, when Mitch slid one hand between them and began to rub her clitoris.

'Oh-h-h—I…' Her words faded into an incoherent babble.

'Open your eyes. Look at me.' His voice was so raw with passion, so deep, she simply did as he'd asked. Commanded.

He smiled at her, his grey-green eyes promising her everything.

One last thrust.

Then her climax crashed through her body. Just as he'd promised—when the storm hit, everything shattered.

And in his eyes she could see the exact moment the storm hit him, too. The same moment everything went wild. The only thing that was real was each other. And they held on very, very tight.

CHAPTER FOUR

MITCH woke early, the next morning, as normal.

Except there was nothing normal about this morning.

Because he was wrapped round a warm, soft, female body.

Jane Redmond.

The woman who'd blown into his life as fast as a storm brewed. And despite her gentle, sweet exterior, she was as dangerous as a tornado. Because, for the first time in years, he'd actually woken up with someone in his arms. Someone he knew instinctively it would be all too easy to let himself care about.

And he couldn't. He really couldn't let himself do that. He'd promised himself that in the dark days after Natalie. He'd never get involved again. Never risk his heart again.

Never.

Besides, he wasn't what Jane needed. Given what she'd told him about her family, it was obvious she wanted someone who'd settle down. Someone who didn't have itchy feet. Someone who wasn't in Iceland one day and Oklahoma the next, literally blowing around the world in the middle of a weather system.

The sensible thing to do would be to ease away from her. Have a cool shower while she slept, to dampen his libido. Dress. Do some work until she woke up, offer her breakfast while being distantly polite and businesslike, and then wave goodbye to her. Within a few minutes she'd be out of his life, and everything could go back to being just the way he liked it.

But he couldn't quite drag himself away from her. Not when her body fitted so perfectly into the curve of his.

So he lay there in the quiet of the early morning, an arm wrapped round her waist to hold her close. Losing himself in the moment—in the scent of her hair, the softness of her skin, the warmth of her body against his—until finally he felt her stir.

'Good morning,' he said softly.

Jane wriggled round in his arms so she was facing him. 'Good morning.'

He scanned her face quickly. No sign of morning-after-itis. No awkwardness, no hope in her eyes that he'd change his mind and ask her to stay—that he'd offer her for ever.

Then again, he had a feeling that Jane Redmond was a woman of her word. And they'd both agreed that yesterday was just one day. She wouldn't expect what he couldn't give her.

'Sleep well?' he asked.

Her eyes were full of laughter as she replied, 'Ish.'

They hadn't actually slept that much. They'd been too busy exploring each other. Finding out where each other liked being touched, being kissed.

She'd found some erogenous zones he hadn't even known he had. Or maybe it was just her.

No.

He wasn't going to let himself think it. This was *over*. One single night. Exactly as they'd agreed.

'What time is it?' she asked.

He leaned over to pick up his watch. 'Nearly seven.'

She nodded. 'I'd better get my skates on, then. I need to get home and change for work.'

She sat up, and he was amused to note that she was holding the duvet across her breasts. Shy? Considering that he'd looked, yesterday… More than looked. Touched. Tasted. Explored every inch of her skin. Lost himself in her warm, sweet depths.

But he rather liked her sense of propriety. The way it drew a line between last night, when they'd let their inhibitions go, and today, when they were going back to their own lives.

'Maybe I'd better text my boss and warn her I might be a little bit late,' she said. 'Um, would you mind passing me my handbag, please?'

It was on the table, on his side of the sofa bed. He passed it to her, and she fished out a mobile phone. Her eyes widened as she flipped up the top. 'Oh, no.'

'What's wrong?'

'I forgot that I switched it off, yesterday. After I, um, took your photo.' She switched it on.

It beeped. Time after time after time.

'That's quite a lot of texts,' he remarked when the beeping finally stopped.

'And voicemails.' She winced as she skimmed through the texts. 'Mainly from my housemates. I really should've phoned home and said I wasn't going to be back, yesterday evening.'

Except they'd distracted each other.

And how.

She pressed a speed-dial button, obviously dialling home. And despite the fact she hadn't switched her phone into speaker mode, Mitch could hear the very second her housemate answered because the shriek was so loud.

'Jane? Jane, are you all right?'

'I'm fine, Charlie.'

'Then where the bloody hell are you?'

Her eyes widened and she looked at Mitch, mouthing, 'Where is this?'

'Harley Street,' he said softly.

'Harley Street,' she repeated into the phone.

'Oh, my God. Are you at some posh doctor's or something? Is there something you haven't told us?'

'Calm down, Charlie. No. I'm not seeing a doctor for anything.'

Hmm. Maybe now wasn't the time to tell her he had a PhD—that he was officially Dr Mitch Holland. He pulled his jockey shorts on, then went over to the little compact kitchen, filled the kettle and spooned instant coffee into two mugs.

'Anyway, I'm too young and too sensible to have come to Harley Street for Botox treatment or what have you. I'm staying at, um, a friend's place. Don't worry. I'm *fine*.'

Charlie's voice had lowered to a more normal tone by now, but Mitch could tell exactly what she was saying from Jane's responses.

'You rang Stella? Why? Oh-h-h. Well, no, I know I didn't tell you I was taking a day off. Because if I had, you'd have asked me why.'

There was a pause.

'Um. I thought you'd forgotten.'

So her housemates *had* remembered her birthday, after all?

Jane was clearly squirming. 'Yes, I know you're not my parents. Yes, I *know* you're my best friends and you wouldn't have forgotten something as important as my twenty-fifth birthday. But, Charlie, you've been under a lot of strain with the reorganisation at work, Hannah's run off her feet at the surgery and Shelley's on the run-up to exams and she's under pressure for her class to perform. Of course I wasn't going to start stomping round the house like a teenager in a strop, asking you all why you'd forgotten my birthday—none of you needed the hassle. I honestly thought you'd all been so busy it had slipped your minds, and I didn't want to make a fuss or make you feel bad.' She sucked in a breath. 'Look, I just decided to have a day doing…' she blushed to the roots of her hair, and Mitch stifled a grin '…things I wouldn't normally do. I climbed the Monument, went to the meridian line and had tea at the Ritz.'

No mention of kissing a stranger, he noticed.

And definitely no mention of what they'd done last night after dinner. All night.

And he really shouldn't be feeling so smug that he'd been the one to introduce her to the concept of the multiple orgasm. This wasn't going any further. He couldn't offer her a future. As she'd said, she was sensible. Her life wouldn't map with his. Words and action. Too far apart.

'You did *what*? Oh, Charlie, I'm so sorry.' Jane drew her knees up to her chin. 'I had no idea. No, none at all.' She looked horror-stricken. 'I'm really sorry I spoiled the surprise.'

He handed her a mug of coffee, and she mouthed her thanks at him before turning her attention back to the phone call.

'No, it was a really lovely thing to do. If I'd guessed… No.' She laughed again. 'Yeah, I know. I'm buried in my old documents and don't notice what's happening under my nose—as bad as my parents and Alex. Uh-huh. OK. I'll see you tonight. Yeah, give them my love. Bye.'

She ended the call and tucked the phone back into her handbag.

Mitch sat on the edge of the bed, cupping his hands round his mug of coffee. 'So what was that all about?'

'My housemates were worried because I'm, um, a bit predictable. So when I disappeared yesterday and didn't tell them I wouldn't be home…' She dragged in a deep breath. 'Charlie rang my boss to see if I'd swapped shifts with someone and was working a late shift—and when she found out I'd booked the day off, she was worried because I hadn't left them a note.' She shrugged. 'I'd intended to be back before any of them came home from work.'

'Except I persuaded you to spend the evening with me instead.'

She nodded. 'And I forgot my phone was switched off, so I didn't pick up their messages. I didn't even think about ringing home.' She bit her lip. 'Hannah rang the emergency department of every hospital in London, in case I'd had an accident. Shelley called the police, except they told her I wouldn't officially be a missing person until today. And I have about a hundred worried messages on my phone.'

'They know you're OK now.'

She nodded. 'But I didn't know they'd planned a surprise party for me."

'So they didn't forget your birthday after all?'

She shook her head. 'I feel horrible. I mean, I know my housemates aren't scatty like my family. They're all really organised and together.'

'But you assumed they'd been busy at work and it'd slipped their minds and you didn't want to put any pressure on them.'

'While they'd secretly been organising this big party, in the function room of the local pub,' she explained. 'Charlie's boyfriend, Luke, plays in a band—they were doing the music, Hannah's mum made the cake and they'd done all the food between them. Everyone had been invited and they'd all been sworn to utter secrecy. They'd beaten me to the post so I'd have a sackful of cards and presents to open on the night.' Jane took a gulp of coffee. 'And then I didn't turn up. Charlie, Hannah and Shelley were going frantic. Oh, God. If only I'd thought to call them yesterday and let them know I wasn't going to come home last night.'

Mitch looked at her over the rim of his mug. 'Don't feel too bad about it.'

She frowned. 'Of course I feel bad about it! They went to a lot of trouble, and I ruined their surprise.'

'But they made you think that they'd forgotten your birthday—they could've told you they were taking you out for a pizza or something, then taken you to the party instead,' he pointed out, 'so you didn't spend the whole day thinking nobody had remembered.'

She made a dismissive movement with her hand. 'I still ruined their surprise. They'd done something really nice for me—they knew I didn't have an eighteenth or a twenty-first party, and they'd been plotting this for months.'

'It's not your fault. You're not a mind-reader.' On impulse, he reached out and touched her cheek. 'Jane. No regrets. That's what we agreed last night.'

'No regrets.' She took a deep breath. 'But I need to go. I'll be late for work.' She handed him her mug; it was still half full. 'And you need to see your agent and catch up with yesterday's meeting.'

'No guilt, either,' he warned.

'No. Um, would you mind…?' She gestured at him to turn his back.

'Hold on.' He fetched the robe from where it was hanging on the bathroom door and handed it to her, then turned his back.

'Thank you,' she said, and he glanced at her to discover her tightly belted into the robe. She fished in the carrier bag and took out clean underwear from the pack she'd bought yesterday, plus the clothes she'd worn during the day. She shook them out and grimaced. 'A bit crumpled, but they're decent enough to get me back home. I'll change for work there,' she said.

He raised both hands in surrender. 'Hey. I'm not commenting on your clothes.' Especially when most of the time he lived in scruffy jeans and an old T-shirt that was washed regularly but didn't even have a nodding acquaintance with an iron. He could barely see a crease in her clothes—what was she on about? 'I'll make us breakfast.'

She shook her head. 'Thanks, but I'm not a breakfast person.'

Although Jane wasn't overweight, she also wasn't the type who spent her time totting up every calorie. She'd eaten with enjoyment yesterday. So was this just an excuse?

She headed for the bathroom; he'd pulled on jeans and a T-shirt and had turned the bed back into an innocuous sofa by the time she emerged. 'At least have another coffee before you go,' he said. Why he was trying to encourage her to stay was completely beyond him. But his mouth just wouldn't stop.

She fastened her watch to her wrist. 'I'm going to be late anyway. Another five minutes isn't going to make much difference.' And then she gave him an impish smile. 'And I'm a much nicer person when you add caffeine.'

He almost told her he liked her *without* the caffeine, too, but he bit the words back. They'd sound too much like an offer. And he couldn't offer her anything. 'Sure you don't want anything to eat? Harry's stocked the fridge with fruit and what have you.'

'Your agent stocked your fridge?'

He wrinkled his nose. 'In storm season, I live on fast food. I love American breakfasts of pancakes and syrup. Sugar overload—Harry nags me over it. So fruit and yoghurt and what have you balances it out when I'm over here.' He opened the fridge. 'Nectarines, strawberries and blueberries. There's a bowl of apples and bananas as well.' He gestured to the worktop. 'And I'm never going to eat all this before I leave. I could do with a hand.'

'You're leaving London today?'

'No, I'm here for a couple more days. Then I need to move on, see some people.' His family. But she didn't need to know that. 'And then I'm back in the States.'

'Chasing tornadoes.'

'Chasing tornadoes,' he confirmed. He took fruit from the fridge, washed it and chopped it, then shared it between two bowls, topping it with plain live yoghurt and a sprinkle of sunflower seeds.

She smiled when he put the bowl on the table in front of her. 'You're well trained. Very healthy.'

He rolled his eyes. 'Harry's good at nagging.'

'Thanks. This is good,' she said after her first mouthful.

And then breakfast was over. Time to say goodbye.

She gathered her bags together. 'Thank you,' she said, 'for yesterday. For making my birthday special.'

'My pleasure.' And it had been. A day for just them. A day without any worries or guilt. A day when he'd been able to breathe.

'Good luck with your exhibition,' she said.

'Thanks. Good luck with facing your housemates.'

'Thanks.' She smiled. 'Well, have a nice life.' She reached up and kissed him lightly on the cheek.

Then the door clicked shut behind her.

He should be relieved. It was what he'd wanted. No tears, no ties. Everything back to normal.

So why did it suddenly feel as if the sun had gone behind a bank of clouds?

'Don't be so soft,' he informed himself loudly. 'You like your life as it is.' OK, so he had a couple of days of awkwardness to get through back in Sussex, but he'd done it before. And it was only for a couple of days.

And then he could get back to the one thing he really loved. The place where he felt safe again.

Tornado Alley.

That evening, once Jane's housemates had hugged her and had satisfied themselves that she was perfectly all right, they made her sit at the kitchen table. Charlie even grabbed a desk-lamp and trained it on her.

'The interrogation starts now. So who was this friend whose place you stayed at last night?' Charlie asked.

Jane made a dismissive motion with her hand. 'Ha, ha. Very funny.'

'We know it was a man, because you've got The Look,' Hannah announced.

Jane frowned. 'What look?' she asked, mystified.

'The look in your eyes that said you had good sex last night, and lots of it,' Charlie said. 'So you've been holding out on us. There's a secret lover, isn't there? And you sneaked out to meet him yesterday.'

Jane felt her face heat. 'Oh, come on.'

'With a blush like that—I reckon you really *did* spend last night having hot sex!' Shelley grinned, opened a bottle of wine and poured it into four glasses, then handed one to each of them. 'Right. Spill the beans, Jane-Jane-Superbrain. We want to know all.'

'No.'

'You had us all worried sick. You *owe* us,' Charlie pointed out.

Jane took a large swig of wine. 'OK. I thought you'd all forgotten my birthday. And I wasn't going to stay in and mope around and have a pity party—I went into town, intending to do some of the things I hadn't got round to doing since I moved to London. Look, I told you about that on the phone this morning.'

'The Monument and tea at the Ritz. Yeah, yeah, yeah,' Charlie said. 'Now give us the real details. Who was this man and where did you meet him?'

'Do I *have* to do this?' Jane asked.

'Yes, you do,' her housemates chorused.

'Or we could just push her face into the cake,' Shelley suggested.

'No, we can't—my mum would have our guts for garters if we wasted her best chocolate cake recipe,' Hannah protested.

A cake that had been made in the shape of an open book, with 'Happy 25th birthday, Jane' iced on it in white chocolate. They'd really made an effort for her.

'It'd be a waste,' Jane agreed. 'And I need cake.'

'Then you have no choice,' Shelley said. 'You have to tell us.'

Against three of them, Jane knew she didn't stand a chance. She sighed. 'OK. Top of my list of things I wanted to do yesterday was kissing a tall, dark, handsome stranger. I saw him on the South Bank.'

Hannah gaped. 'You went up to a total stranger and snogged him?'

Jane shuffled in her seat. 'No. I chickened out. I took his photo and he saw me. We had coffee and I told him about my list of things, so he suggested joining me on the day.'

Charlie's eyes narrowed. 'What kind of man can just take a day off when he feels like it, with no notice?'

'He's self-employed.'

'Doing what?' Charlie asked.

'What is this—twenty questions?' Jane prevaricated.

'Good idea,' Shelley said. 'Question one. What does he do?'

Oh, hell. She'd really started something now. Jane was tempted to fib, but she knew she was a hopeless liar. It was better to be honest right from the start. Tell the truth—but maybe not *all* the truth. 'He's a stormchaser.'

Shelley blinked. 'A *what*?'

'That's question two. Same answer,' Jane said quickly. 'He chases storms.' The expressions on their faces told her she needed to elaborate. 'He takes photographs of extreme weather.'

'Tornadoes and that? Then he's a thrill-seeker. One of these people who take outrageous risks and get off on it. You went off with a *maniac*!' Hannah accused.

'He wasn't a maniac. He was very nice.' Just how nice, she wasn't prepared to admit.

'Tall, dark and handsome,' Charlie mused. 'How handsome? Oh, and that's question three.'

'Very.'

'Not specific enough,' Charlie said. 'Between one and ten, where is he on the scale of handsomeness?'

Jane blew out a breath. 'I'd say ten and a half.'

'Where's the photo?' Charlie asked.

Jane took her mobile phone from her bag and flicked through the photographs until she reached the one of Mitch. 'Here.'

Charlie whistled. 'Definitely ten and a half.'

'So are you seeing him again?' Shelley asked.

Jane shook her head. 'It was just for one day.'

'And night,' Hannah pointed out.

Charlie folded her arms. 'So you're telling us that you—the sensible one in the house—went off and had a one-night stand with a total stranger?'

Jane groaned. 'Oh, for goodness' sake. Anyone would think I was one of Stella's teenage daughters getting the third degree for coming home after midnight!'

'You didn't come home at all,' Charlie said with a grin. 'And your boss practically thinks of you as one of her kids, so consider us a substitute for Stella.'

'She didn't grill me this morning the way you're grilling me now,' Jane protested.

Charlie adjusted the light. 'Well, I happen to think this *deserves* interrogation.'

'Because we're worried about you. You don't just stay out all night without telling one of us where you're going,' Shelley said.

'Particularly,' Hannah added, 'when he's a total stranger. You could've got into serious trouble.'

Jane shook her head. 'My instincts said not.'

'Jane, honey, your instincts are sh—' Shelley clapped her hand in front of her mouth. 'Um. Let me rephrase that. You're not street-savvy like our Charlie, so I wouldn't rely on your instincts.'

'Look, would an axe-murderer take me out to dinner to a seriously exclusive restaurant?'

'Maybe. If he was rich. Or he could be a fraudster—he might have stolen someone's identity and credit card details,' Hannah said. 'You might find he's cloned your credit card and, wham, next bill, you'll have thousands of pounds notched up to your account from somewhere in Asia.'

Jane frowned. 'Don't be ridiculous.'

'Cloning happens,' Charlie said thoughtfully. 'One of my friends got caught out at a petrol station. Luckily the credit-card company rang her when the third charge came through and asked if she'd lost her card or something.'

'Look, he's not a fraudster.' Jane shook her head. 'He was a perfect gentleman.'

Charlie coughed. 'Right. And perfect gentlemen have one-night stands.'

'It was by mutual agreement. I'm not looking for a relationship. Well, not unless that Hollywood actor I love proposes to me,' Jane added with a grin.

'That's not going to happen.' Charlie smiled with a dismissive wave of her hand. 'So. You had a one-night stand with a total stranger.'

'All right,' Jane said, spreading her hands. 'How many times are you going to ask me?'

Hannah grinned. 'Was he good?'

Jane couldn't help laughing. 'I am *not* telling you every single detail.'

'Spoilsport.' Charlie wrinkled her nose. 'Seriously. We've been feeling really bad about yesterday, Jane. It didn't occur to us you might think we'd forgotten your birthday. We were so sure you'd guess we were planning something—especially as I'd got up early all week to grab the post and hide your cards and parcels.'

Charlie was most definitely not a morning person, so Jane knew that'd taken a real effort on her part.

'And I hate to think you spent the day thinking nobody loved you,' Charlie continued, 'when we all do. To bits.'

Jane's heart melted. 'I know that. I just… Look, I'm sorry I messed up your surprise. And I bought chocolates to apologise.'

'No need for that,' Hannah said softly. 'As long as you're OK, that's all we care about.'

'No, no, no, no, no,' Shelley said, wagging her finger. 'I had the day from hell. I'm not turning down chocolate. Though what Hannah said's right,' she added.

Hannah flapped a hand at Charlie. 'Turn that light off. Interrogation over.' She smiled at Jane. 'So did you have a good birthday?'

Jane nodded.

Charlie gave her a wicked smile. 'He made you come, then.'

'Interrogation over,' Jane pointed out. 'The light's off. And are you going to continue torturing me with that cake or please can I have some now?'

'Pudding before dinner? Tut-tut,' Shelley said.

'Considering you eat chocolate for breakfast, you've got room to talk. *Not,*' Jane retorted. 'I claim belated birthday rights. Cake first.'

'All right, all right. Seeing as you bought chocolate as well.' Hannah cut four generous slices.

Jane took a bite. 'Oh-h-h. This is wonderful. Hannah, tell your mum she makes the best chocolate cake in the world.'

'The question is, is chocolate better than sex?' Charlie asked.

'That depends,' Jane said. 'I'm not telling. No more questions.'

Hannah gave her a hug. 'One last one. But this is important. If you're going to have sex with a stranger,' she said, 'it'd better be worth it. And please tell me you were sensible.'

Jane rolled her eyes. 'Hannah, you're a practice nurse who spends too much time with teenagers. You nag us all and make us carry condoms with us. So yes. Of *course* we used condoms.' A lot of them. Some had been his, some hers.

'Good.' Shelley smiled at her. 'Now, since you're having cake before dinner—pressies, too?'

Jane beamed. 'I thought you'd never ask!'

She was so lucky, she realised. Living in a house in Old Isleworth with three brilliant housemates—the warmth of the friendship between them made up for the fact that her room was tiny and furthest from the bathroom. They looked out for each other, shared the good times as well as the bad, and life couldn't get any better than this.

Well, unless Mitch Holland was around.

But they'd already agreed that wasn't going to happen, so she wasn't going to let herself moon over him. She was just going to enjoy being twenty-five, free and single.

CHAPTER FIVE

THREE weeks. It had been practically three weeks since they'd spent the night together, and Jane was still thinking about Mitch.

Pa-a-a-thetic.

If he'd wanted to see her again, he would've tried to track her down. And it wouldn't have been that difficult: he already knew what she did for a living and that she'd worked on the pirate exhibition. A couple of phone calls would've netted him her contact details. The fact that he hadn't even tried made it obvious that she really did have more chance of marrying her favourite film star than of seeing Mitch Holland again. So she really ought to get him out of her head.

And maybe that prawn mayonnaise sandwich yesterday hadn't been a good idea. She'd been feeling queasy all morning.

She was still feeling rough, two days later. And when Jane picked at her toast that morning, Hannah took her to one side before she left for work.

'You're not OK—your face is practically green—so you can stop being brave about it,' Hannah said gently. 'What's wrong?'

'That prawn sandwich must have disagreed with me,' Jane said.

'Yesterday?'

'Three days ago.'

Hannah frowned. 'Food poisoning's usually over in a couple of days. Is there a stomach bug going round at work?'

'Not as far as I know,' Jane said.

Hannah laid her hand on Jane's forehead. 'Not hot enough for me to get the thermometer. So what are your symptoms?'

Typical Hannah: bringing her work home with her. Though it felt good to be fussed over. 'I just feel a bit sick. And kitchen smells make me queasy.' Jane shrugged. 'As I said, it was probably that prawn sandwich.'

'Have you actually been sick?'

'No.'

Hannah looked thoughtful. 'Have you found yourself weeing more often than usual?'

Jane thought about it. 'Yes, a bit,' she admitted. 'Why?'

Hannah blew out a breath. 'Have you considered the fact you might be pregnant?'

Jane rolled her eyes. 'Don't be daft. Of course I'm not. We used condoms.'

'But no contraception is a hundred per cent guaranteed—well, except abstinence,' Hannah said. 'There's still a risk, even with a condom. They can tear, or spill while one of you removes it. These things happen. And it only takes one little sperm to fertilise an egg.'

'Oh, my God.' Jane clapped a hand to her mouth. 'I can't be pregnant.'

'When was your last period?'

Ice trickled down Jane's spine as she counted mentally. 'Five weeks ago. Oh, my God. I'm late.'

'OK. You're busy at work so it might be stress making you late. And it's possible to skip a period for a number of reasons. But you need to get a test kit today so we can start ruling out the possibilities,' Hannah said quietly.

Jane bit her lip. 'Hannah, can we keep this just between you and me for the moment, please?'

'Sure.'

Jane hugged her. 'Thanks, I really appreciate what you're doing for me.'

'It's probably a false alarm. But it's better to know for sure,' Hannah said.

Jane could barely concentrate at work all morning. At lunchtime, she visited a chemist she didn't normally go to, and picked up a pregnancy test. A test she couldn't bring herself to do at work; it sat accusingly at the back of a drawer, wrapped in a plain paper bag, all afternoon.

And then it was time to go home. Time to find out.

Was she pregnant?

When she walked into the kitchen, Hannah was doing a crossword at the table. She looked up. 'Did you do it?'

'Not yet. But here's the test.'

'Just to save you reading the instructions, they're pretty standard. You just take the cap off and wee onto the end of the stick. A blue line in one window shows you the test has worked. If the other window stays blank, you're not pregnant and it might be some kind of bug that's making you feel rough.'

Jane forced herself to ask the question. 'And if it's not a bug?'

'Then you'll see a blue line in the other window, too.' Hannah paused. 'It might be fainter than the first line, but that'll still be a positive result.'

Jane dragged in a breath. 'Right.'

'Stop fretting and just go and do it,' Hannah said. 'I'll make you a mug of hot water with lemon—if it's a bug, it'll help your stomach, and if it's not…well, it'll help the nausea.'

Three minutes later, Jane walked back into the kitchen, holding the little stick.

'Well?'

Numbly, Jane put the stick into her friend's hand.

Hannah looked at it. 'Two lines.' She stood up and gave Jane a hug. 'That's pretty conclusive, hon.'

'I—I can't be.'

Hannah said nothing, but she didn't have to. The two lines said it all.

Jane was pregnant.

With Mitch's baby.

'What the hell am I going to do?' she whispered.

'Come and sit down.' Hannah shepherded her over to a chair, then gave her the hot drink. 'This will help.'

'Thanks, Hannah.' Jane stared at the cup. 'I can't believe this. I just…'

'Right now you're in shock,' Hannah said. 'It's a lot to take in, but you're not the first to have an unplanned pregnancy and you won't be the last.' She paused. 'You don't have to make any decisions yet. It's still early stages. But you do need to talk it over with your stormchaser. Do you have his number? His business card?'

Jane shook her head. 'It was only ever meant to be for one night. Just one single night. And no ties.'

'Looks as if that one's backfired a bit.' Hannah squeezed her hand. 'OK, so you probably can't expect any support from that quarter. That's not a problem—you've got your family and you've got us. And Charlie and Shelley and I will support you in whatever decision you make. But you do need to talk to him before you decide anything.' Before Jane could protest, Hannah added softly, 'I've seen enough women who fell pregnant accidentally, didn't talk it over with the father before making a decision, and never got over the guilt. You need to talk it through with him. Find out how he feels about the situation.'

'I don't even know how to get in touch with him.'

Hannah raised an eyebrow. 'You help people trace their ancestors. Surely it's easier to find someone who's alive now than to find someone who lived years and years ago?' She smiled. 'Besides, we have a secret weapon. Charlie.'

Right on cue, Charlie walked into the kitchen. 'Are you talking about me?'

'Not yet,' Hannah said with a grin.

Charlie peered into their mugs. 'Hot water and lemon? Oh, revolting. Don't tell me you're on some kind of detox, Jane?'

'Not exactly,' Jane muttered.

Charlie frowned. 'What's going on?'

In answer, Jane handed her the test stick.

Charlie's eyes widened. 'Oh, blimey. What are you going to do?'

Jane wrapped her arms round herself. 'Right now, I don't know. I can't quite take it in.'

'You need to talk to him,' Charlie said decisively.

'That's what Hannah says, too.' Jane bit her lip. 'But I don't have any way of getting in contact with him.'

'Yes, you do.' Charlie ruffled her hair. 'Don't tell me preggy brain starts this early on, Hannah?'

Hannah laughed. 'No.'

'Just think, when the hormones kick in you might become a normal person instead of Jane-Jane-Superbrain,' Charlie teased.

'I don't feel very brainy right now,' Jane said wryly.

'This doesn't have anything to do with your brain or hormones, hon. It's panic. I'm going to get my lappie and we'll sort this out.' Charlie returned a couple of minutes later with her laptop, set it on the kitchen table where all three of them could see it, and switched it on. 'Right. We'll Google him.'

Jane groaned. 'Why didn't I think of that?'

'Because you're still in shock,' Hannah said.

'So what's his name?' Charlie asked.

'Mitch Holland.'

Charlie tapped the name into the search engine, then stared at the results. 'We need to narrow this down. Right. He's a stormchaser, you said?'

'And he takes photographs. He's setting up some kind of exhibition,' Jane confirmed.

'Well, there you go. Find the exhibition and we find him. It's in London?'

Jane shook her head. 'I don't know, but his meeting was.'

'OK. We'll start with London, and expand the search out if we have to.' She tapped a few more keys, then grinned. 'Bingo. Found him. Pen? Paper?'

Hannah grabbed the box of sticky notes and the pen from beside the kitchen phone, and passed them across to Charlie, who made a note of the art gallery name and the exhibition's opening hours.

'What's this? Checking to see what's on at the cinema tonight so we can have a girly night out?' Shelley asked, coming in to find them huddled over the computer.

Jane explained.

'Oh, Janey.' Shelley hugged her. 'You definitely need to go and see him. We'll go with you.'

'Absolutely. And if he's anything other than a hundred per cent nice about it, Shelley can lecture him, I can practise my martial arts on him, and Hannah can patch up his bruises afterwards,' Charlie added.

Jane smiled wryly at the picture. 'It's hardly fair to unleash a posse on the poor guy. It isn't his fault.'

'It's not exclusively yours, either,' Hannah pointed out. 'It takes two to make a baby.'

'And you need moral support,' Shelley added.

'If it worries you that much, we'll melt into the background when you see him, but we're coming with you,' Charlie informed her.

'There's no need. I'll be fine,' Jane said.

'Don't argue. You're taking one of us, and that's not negotiable.' Charlie grabbed her handbag and took a coin from her purse. 'Right. Hannah—heads or tails?'

'Heads.'

Charlie tossed the coin. 'Tails—I win. Shelley?'

'Tails.'

A second toss of the coin. 'Heads. I win again. So I'm coming with you, Jane.'

'Are these his photographs?' Shelley asked, looking at the samples on the screen. 'They're really good. I love that one of the lightning.'

'And have you seen that one of the tornado? Incredible,' Charlie said. 'And it's a bit scary that he got that close to the thing.' And then she switched to another page on the website—one with a photograph of Mitch.

Clearly he'd just finished chasing a storm, Jane thought, because he was dressed in a faded T-shirt, scruffy jeans and a leather jacket. He needed a shave. But he was smiling—just as he had when they'd made love. And he looked as sexy as hell. Her whole body tingled with the memories and she sucked in a breath. 'How on earth am I going to tell him the news?'

'Coolly, calmly and professionally. Just like you are at work when someone's researching their family tree and finds something that upsets them—you know you're good at that,' Shelley said.

'Stella's always singing your praises about how brilliant you are with people,' Hannah added.

'We'll go tomorrow,' Charlie said. 'It's Saturday so that's just about perfect. We'll have lunch to fortify ourselves—'

'Because no way will Charlie be up in time for breakfast on a Saturday,' Shelley chipped in.

Charlie just spread her hands. 'I can get up if I have to. But lunch sounds good. And then we'll go see your stormchaser. I'll stay out of the way while you're talking to him—but I'll keep you in sight. All you have to do is raise your little finger if you're in trouble, and I'll be straight there to bail you out.'

Jane felt her lower lip wobble. 'Thanks, all of you. I…' To her horror, she burst into tears.

Hannah gave her a hug. 'Now *that's* hormones working. But don't worry, Jane. Everything's going to be fine.'

Jane wasn't so sure. But one thing she did know; she couldn't take the coward's way out.

Which meant talking to Mitch.

The following afternoon, after a lunch where Jane felt too sick to eat more than the dry crust of a sandwich, she and Charlie walked into the exhibition.

Mitch was nowhere to be seen, but Jane wasn't that surprised. He'd already told her that he got stir-crazy when he was stuck indoors. Besides, it was the weekend. He probably had better things to do. And he might not even be in the country. He might be chasing a storm somewhere.

'If he's not here, we need to find his agent,' Charlie said. 'I didn't think to Google that before we left. Do you have a name?'

'Just a first name. Harry.'

'Harry. Well, it'll do for a start. We'll ask at the reception desk. And if he isn't here, we'll get his address and go on Monday morning.' Charlie marched Jane over to the desk, then prodded her.

'Excuse me, please. Can you tell me where I can find Harry, Mr Holland's agent?' Jane asked politely.

The girl behind the desk smiled. 'Over there.' She indicated a group of people standing by one of the photographs, a shot of a double rainbow over a canyon.

Jane was about to ask which one was Harry when the phone rang, and the receptionist answered it. Jane waited a moment or so until it was clear that it would be a long phone call, then sighed. 'Oh, well. I can't feel much more awkward than I do already. So I raise my little finger if I get stuck, yes?' she said to Charlie.

'I'll come with you, if you want,' Charlie offered.

Jane shook her head. 'Thanks, but I ought to stand on my own two feet.' Her feet felt like two lumps of lead, but she made herself walk over to the group at a normal pace.

'Excuse me for interrupting, but which of you is Harry, please?'

'I am.'

Jane blinked. From what Mitch had said, she'd expected Harry to be around fifty, male, and very probably gay. Not a woman who looked only a couple of years older than Jane herself, dressed in a sharp business suit and with blonde hair cut in a very trendy style.

'Can I help you?' Harry asked.

'I...um...wondered if I could have a word, please.'

Harry looked her up and down, then nodded. 'See you in a minute, guys,' she said, and drew Jane off to the side. 'So what can I do for you?'

'I...' Jane shook her head. 'Sorry. I'm not normally this clueless. But when Mitch said his agent was called Harry...'

'You were expecting a man,' Harry finished with a wry smile. 'It's short for Harriet. Though Mitch has been known to change it to "harridan" before now.' She gave Jane a curious look. 'So you're the reason why he didn't come back to that meeting, the other week?'

Jane really hadn't expected that. 'He told you about me?'

Harry shook her head. 'But with Mitch it isn't what he says that's important. It's what he doesn't say.'

Jane didn't have a clue what he'd say when he heard her news. Or what he wouldn't say. She'd spent a day and a night with him, and he was still a complete stranger.

And the father of her unborn child.

She took a deep breath. 'I need to talk to him.'

'Can I help?' Harry asked.

Jane shook her head. 'It's personal.'

'Personal,' Harry said dryly.

'Look, I'm not a stalker. But this...' She shook her head. 'I need to talk to him about it. Preferably face to face. Is he even in the country at the moment?'

'Maybe, maybe not.' Harry's face was unreadable.

'I understand that you need to protect his interests,' Jane said softly, 'but this is something he really needs to know about. And he needs to hear it from *me*.'

Harry frowned. 'I don't like the sound of this.'

'I'm not going to make trouble,' Jane said. It wasn't strictly true: she didn't *intend* to cause trouble, but she had no idea how Mitch was going to react to the news. She took a business card from her handbag and handed it to Harry. 'Here. If you want to check me out, this is as good a place as any to start. But please—please ask Mitch to call me. It's really important.'

The silence stretched until Jane was almost at screaming point.

And then Harry nodded, handing the card back to her. 'OK. Write your home and mobile numbers on the back. If you check out then I'll get him to call you.'

'Thank you,' Jane said, scribbled down her number, then forced herself to smile and rejoin Charlie.

'Well?' Charlie asked.

Jane filled her in on what Harry had said.

'It's a waiting game, then. Still, at least it'll give you time to get your head straight. Work out what to say to him,' Charlie said. 'While we're here, we might as well look round the exhibition.'

'Sure,' Jane said.

The photographs were incredible; they had the same restless energy as Mitch himself did. Though it also told her something else: Mitch was like her parents and her brother, always needing to be on the move. Just as they'd go from site to site and lecture tour to lecture tour, Mitch would go from storm to storm.

Exactly what she grew up with.

Exactly what she didn't want to spend the rest of her life with—assuming that was even an option.

But right now she couldn't assume anything. She'd just have to wait until Harry passed on the message—and hope that Mitch would call her.

* * *

The following Tuesday, Jane's mobile phone rang. She glanced at the screen but didn't recognise the number.

Mitch?

She damped down the hope. It was probably a cold caller. But she answered anyway. 'Hello?'

'Jane, it's Mitch. Harry gave me your number.'

Straight and to the point. Oh, God.

'So what did you want to talk to me about?'

How the hell did she tell him? She swallowed. 'This needs to be in person.'

'Why?'

She dragged in a breath. 'Because it's…personal.' She had to get control of the situation. 'Can we meet up?'

'When?'

She couldn't tell a thing from his tone. 'Tomorrow?'

'It'll have to be the evening.' There was a pause, as if he was checking his schedule. 'Half six?'

'That's fine. Um…where's convenient for you?'

'I'm on the Circle line right now. Great Portland Street. You?'

'District. Richmond.'

'So halfway would be…let me see…South Kensington. Not the tube station, because it'd be too easy to miss each other. I'll see you on the front steps of the Natural History Museum.'

Well, she should have expected briskness. The man chased storms. He was used to navigating fast.

But some kind of personal thing would've been nice. He hadn't even asked her how she was. He was back to being the forbidding stranger she'd been too chicken to kiss on the South Bank—not the man who'd made her laugh round half of London and who'd made her see stars when they'd made love. 'OK,' she said, knowing this wasn't going to be OK at all.

And although she managed to get through the next day at work, she felt more and more nervous, the nearer she got to

South Kensington. Bile rose in her stomach, and she wasn't sure if it was fear or morning sickness. All-day sickness, more like: the nausea came and went. And it wasn't helped by the stuffiness on the train, either. She took a bottle of plain water from her bag and sipped it. Small, frequent sips had been Hannah's advice. And it did help. A bit.

But when the train stopped and she headed through the underground passage towards the museums, her heart was beating madly and adrenalin made her fingers feel stiff. She could hear a busker playing 'Yesterday' on the cello, the music growing louder as she walked towards him; the rich, deep sweetness of the notes echoing in the tunnel made the tune sound even more melancholy. And right at that moment she could really identify with the words of the song. She'd like somewhere to hide away, too, instead of having to face Mitch with what she knew would be unwelcome news.

When she emerged onto the road and walked down the slope leading to the gardens of the museum, she could see Mitch sitting on the steps outside the building. Looking as gorgeous as she remembered him—her heart missed a beat—but remote and untouchable, despite the fact that he was wearing faded jeans.

Please let this not be as bad as she feared.

Mitch noticed that Jane wasn't smiling, though she raised her hand in acknowledgement as soon as she saw him. And he had the feeling that he really wasn't going to like whatever she was intending to tell him. *Personal.* A number of possibilities had gone through his mind—and none of them had left him smiling.

Better get this over with.

He stood up and walked to meet her.

What now?

They were well past the handshaking stage, but kissing

her didn't feel right either. So he jammed his hands in his pockets. 'Hello.'

'Hello.' She looked nervous. And slightly pale, as if she had a headache.

'Shall we sit down?' He indicated the empty bench nearby.

'Sure.'

They sat down in silence. And her nervousness had communicated itself to him: although he tried for casual, stretching his legs out and leaning back, he found himself jiggling one foot.

The silence went on and on and on, to the point where it was unbearable.

Clearly he'd have to be the one to break it. 'So what did you want to see me about?'

She swallowed hard. 'There isn't an easy way to say this.'

He shrugged. 'Tell me straight, then.'

'I'm pregnant.'

Time stopped.

Blood roared in his ears.

And the words echoed in his head. *I'm pregnant.*

In a different voice. Not Jane's. *We're going to have a baby.*

No, no, no, no, no.

This couldn't be happening.

He must be hallucinating. Please, let him be hallucinating. 'Could you repeat that?' he asked.

Her voice quivered slightly as she replied, 'I'm pregnant.'

'You can't be.' He shook his head. 'You *can't* be.'

Her face was very pale. 'I took a test last week.'

Even so. Tests could be wrong, couldn't they? 'We were careful. We used condoms.' And he knew damn well he'd used them properly. No way should she be pregnant.

'According to my housemate Hannah—who's a practice nurse, so I'd say she knows what she's talking about—condoms are pretty safe but there's still a small failure rate.'

'If you don't use them properly. But we didn't take a single risk.' He'd been meticulous about it. He always was, nowadays. Much as he'd wanted to feel the heat of her body wrapped round him, he'd exercised control. Made sure they were protected. 'How could a condom have failed?'

'I don't know.' She folded her arms and turned away from him slightly: defensive body language in the extreme.

I'm pregnant. The words churned in the pit of his stomach. 'This can't be happening.'

'I'm not wonderfully happy about it, either.'

'So what are you going to do?'

'I thought you had the right to know, before any decisions were made.' A muscle flickered in her jaw. 'I suppose I should be grateful you haven't asked if I'm sure it's yours.'

That hadn't even occurred to him. But now she'd raised it… 'Is it?' She flinched as if he'd hit her, and he immediately felt contrite. 'I'm sorry. I didn't mean that.'

'I don't sleep around.' Her voice was prickly with hurt.

Oh, hell. He could see her eyes filling with tears. He was just glad he was wearing dark glasses so she couldn't see his own eyes. So she didn't see the pain of his memories.

'I apologise.'

She didn't say anything, but to his relief she rubbed the back of her hand over her eyes and squished the tears.

She was pregnant.

With his baby.

This moment should be a celebration of new life.

But he'd been here before

And crashed and burned.

Never, ever again was he going to let himself be put in that situation.

He was aware that his fists were clenched so hard, his knuckles stood out in sharp white relief, and he forced himself to relax his hands. Jane wasn't to know what had happened. It wasn't her fault. But no way was he getting involved. 'If you decide to keep the baby, then I'll support you financially.' He'd do the right thing. From a distance. 'Just let Harry know your bank details and she'll arrange it all.'

'So that's *it*? This is just a financial transaction?'

Again, he was glad of the dark glasses. Because he didn't want her to see his eyes, guess what was going on in his head. Didn't want to talk about it. Because it hurt too much to think about the past. About the might-have-beens. 'I was honest with you right from the start. I'm not looking for a relationship. Of any sort. And I'm going away again anyway. There's no point in dragging this out.'

'So you want nothing to do with the baby.'

The baby. Oh, God. The baby. His child. He swallowed. 'No.'

'Then I want nothing to do with your money. Goodbye.' Her mouth tightened, and she turned on her heel and left.

And that was it.

Problem solved.

Except he knew it wasn't. He knew he'd handled this badly. Hurt her.

But what other choice did he have?

CHAPTER SIX

'HE SAID *what*?' Charlie demanded, outraged. 'That's... that's...' Her mouth opened and closed and she shook her head, clearly at a loss.

'That's about the first time ever you've been lost for words,' Jane said wryly. 'Look, forget it. I am. He's not worth it.' She really hoped her voice sounded cool and calm and unruffled. Even though her heart felt as if it had just been through the shredder. The man she'd spent the night with was warm and fun and sexy. The man she'd faced outside the museum had been cold, hard and unfeeling—a complete stranger.

More fool her for hoping for something more.

'So what do you want to do, Jane?' Shelley asked, squeezing her hand. 'You know you've got our support, whatever you decide.'

'I've been thinking about it. Asking myself over and over again.' Losing sleep over it. Trying to second-guess Mitch's reaction—but even so she hadn't been prepared for it. Or for how much it had hurt her. 'I'm twenty-five, with a career that's just starting to go in the direction I want it to. Being a single parent is going to change all that—I'd have to make a hell of a lot of compromises—and bringing up a baby on my own isn't going to be easy.' She bit her lip. 'But I can't face the alternative. I'm not condemning people who make that decision. It's a very, very hard one to make and you need to be very sure what you're doing. But…' she shook her head '…it's not what I want.'

'So you're going to keep the baby?' Hannah asked.

Jane nodded. 'I realise I'll have to find somewhere else to li—'

'Don't be daft,' Charlie cut in. 'We might have to rearrange the house a bit, but you're not going to move out just because you're pregnant. Anyway, it's going to be an awful lot easier babysitting if you're living here rather than having to drag ourselves over to some damp, horrible little poky flat somewhere.'

Jane knew her friend was just trying to make her feel better. 'What about if the baby cries in the night?'

'Charlie sleeps through thunderstorms,' Shelley pointed out, 'I'm used to babies crying in the playground right outside my classroom door, and Hannah's used to babies in the surgery. We won't hear a thing—and if we do we'll tune it out.'

'Besides, it's only a few months until they get into a routine of sleeping through the night,' Hannah said. 'And it'd be nice to have a baby around.'

'You know, babies are seriously trendy fashion accessories. We can borrow him or her and pretend we're Yummy Mummies,' Charlie said with a grin.

Jane stared at them, not sure whether to laugh or cry.

Hannah patted her shoulder. 'Bottom line, hon, you're staying—and we're going to enjoy being disreputable aunties.'

'Agreed,' Shelley said.

At the same time as Charlie added, 'No arguments.'

Jane blinked back the tears. 'You three are just…you're the best. And my baby's so lucky to have three such wonderful women in his or her life. You will all be godmothers, won't you?'

'Sure,' Charlie said, affecting a nonchalant air. But Jane could see the glimmer of tears in her friend's eyes.

'Well, as the nurse in the house, I'm taking charge of antenatal stuff,' Hannah said.

'And as the teacher in the house, I'm in on the educational toy front,' Shelley chipped in.

'Which leaves me as style queen—so I'll take you shopping for baby clothes and the coolest pushchair in town,' Charlie said. 'Good. Sorted. Now—time for cake, I think...'

The first antenatal check wasn't as bad as Jane expected. Her housemates were the most brilliant support team in the world. She didn't need Mitch Holland. At all.

But even so, when she got the letter with the date for her first scan, something prompted her to text him. Just to let him know what was happening.

He didn't reply. Ha. Well, not that she'd expected him to. He'd made it pretty clear that he didn't want anything to do with the baby. His silence just underlined it. There was no point in moping about it; being miserable wouldn't make him change his mind. Though his refusal even to acknowledge his child stung. And her disappointment must have been obvious when Hannah went to the scan with her, because Hannah squeezed her hand as they walked into the hospital. 'Are you OK?'

'Sure,' Jane fibbed.

Hannah sighed. 'No, you're not. You wish the baby's dad was here with you, don't you?'

Just like her other housemates, Hannah refused to use Mitch's name. Though at least she'd kept a neutral version. Charlie's name for him was much, much ruder. Jane forced herself to smile. 'You swapped your shift to be here with me today. And I really, really appreciate that.'

'Even so. Maybe you should have another word with this Harry person. She might make him face up towards his responsibilities.'

'It's not going to happen,' Jane said, 'and there's no point in setting myself up for disappointment. I'll be fine.'

But a few minutes later, when the radiographer spread the

radioconductive gel over Jane's abdomen and then showed her the reading on the screen, tears welled in her eyes. 'My baby,' she whispered.

'Here's an arm, here's the other one, here are the legs, and here's the spine,' the radiographer said with a smile. 'All looking good.' She made a few measurements on screen. 'And from this I'd say you're bang on twelve weeks. The baby's due in the second week of January.'

'A late Christmas pressie,' Hannah said with a smile. 'One definitely worth waiting for.'

'Would you like a photograph?' the radiographer asked.

'Oh, yes. Please.' Jane beamed at her. 'Is it possible to have more than one copy, please?'

'No problem.'

Armed with half a dozen copies of the scan photograph, she went back to work. She scanned in the picture during her lunch break and sent a copy by email to Charlie, who she knew would pick it up at work, and another to Shelley's phone.

Should she send one to Mitch?

She suppressed the idea immediately. He'd made it clear he didn't want to know. So she wasn't going to brood and wish that things were different; she was just going to enjoy her pregnancy. She could relax, secure in the knowledge that everything was fine. And now she had dates and confirmation that all was well, she could ring her parents and her brother tonight—if she could actually get hold of them in the remote area where they were working right now—and break the news to them.

Charlie rang her straight away. 'Congratulations! Jane, that's an amazing picture. We're toasting you in champagne tonight.'

'That'd better be iced water for me.'

'No worries. I'm sure the three of us can cope with your share of the bubbly,' Charlie said, laughing. 'Hey—guess what? I'm going to be an aunty! Yeehah!'

* * *

Three days.

It had been three days since Jane had been due to have the scan.

And she hadn't contacted him. Hadn't told him if everything was all right.

Nausea coiled in Mitch's stomach. He wasn't supposed to feel like this. He'd walked away and she'd told him she wanted nothing from him. He was supposed to be getting on with his job, his life. Not thinking about the baby.

But the memories crowded back. Memories of when his world had crashed, broken into tiny shards, two years before. And he couldn't shake the fear that it was about to happen all over again. That Jane—Jane, who'd managed to make him forget for a whole day and night—would…

No.

He couldn't bear this.

Not again.

'Are you OK?' Brad, one of his colleagues, asked, poking his head through the open window of the pick-up.

Mitch's head jerked back so fast that he cracked it against the back of his seat. 'Sure,' he lied.

'I don't know if you've been having a nap or something, but I've been trying to patch someone through on the radio.'

His mother, about to break the same news to him that she'd had to break two years ago?

No, of course not. She didn't even know Jane existed.

He really had to get a grip and stop being so paranoid. What had happened to Natalie was rare. *Really* rare. It didn't automatically mean that the same thing would happen to Jane.

But the fear and the nausea wouldn't go away.

If anything, the coils were getting tighter. To the point where it was a physical pain.

'Are you *sure* you're OK? You look a bit—'

'I'm fine,' Mitch said curtly. 'Patch whoever it is through.'

He relaxed when he heard a voice he recognised. Work. A

simple question. Nothing to worry about. He dealt with it, but then he slid back into brooding.

Was Jane all right?

Was there something wrong—with her or with the baby?

Eventually, he pulled his mobile phone out of his pocket and typed in a brief message.

How did the scan go? You OK? M.

He ignored the fact that he didn't even have to look up her number—despite the fact that he hadn't programmed it into his phone.

And then he slid the phone back into his pocket and tried to get on with some work. She'd answer soon enough.

But she didn't.

When he caught himself glancing at his watch for the fiftieth time, he scowled. 'Get a grip,' he told himself. Of course she wouldn't reply immediately. Right then it was eleven in the morning in Kansas. London was six hours ahead, so Jane was probably still at work. There wouldn't be any reception for her mobile phone on the tube, so she might not pick up his text until she got home. He shouldn't expect to hear anything until at least two o'clock, his time.

But two came and went, and still his phone didn't beep.

No messages.

It got to six. Midnight in London: Jane would be asleep, by now.

Maybe his message hadn't got through.

Maybe he should try again.

Or maybe he shouldn't.

Three hours later, he cracked and texted again. It was three in the morning, her time, so he wouldn't hear before midnight, his time, at the earliest.

But there was nothing at midnight.

He switched his light off but lay awake, just waiting for the quiet beep that would signal her reply. Although he dozed fitfully, he didn't hear a thing. Just kept glancing at the dim light of the clock, watching the numbers flash by with each passing minute.

Was she OK?

Or was the whole nightmare happening all over again?

Jane stared at her phone.

Two messages from Mr 'I don't want to be involved'.

Had it been just one message, she could have put it down to him trying to salve his conscience—he knew that he'd behaved like a total louse but probably thought that sending a text asking if she and the baby were OK was enough.

But then to send a second text…

It sounded as if he really did want to know. As if he *meant* it. As if he was worried about her.

OK, so he hadn't bothered to contact her before the scan. But maybe he'd been in some place where there wasn't a phone signal. Despite her best efforts, a tiny flicker of hope glowed in her heart. Maybe he'd had time to think about the situation. To realise that he wasn't the only one involved, here. And maybe the man she'd made love with—the man she'd laughed with—would triumph over the cold, bitter stranger who'd offered her financial support at a distance.

But she didn't reply immediately.

Because how did she know she could trust him not to blow cold again? Maybe she'd be better off deleting the texts and ignoring them. Then again, this wasn't just about her. The baby had rights, too. Who was she to deny the baby its right to some sort of contact with its father?

She thought about it all morning.

Finally, at the end of her lunch break, she replied.

* * *

The alarm beeped. Mitch slammed it off. For a moment, he pulled the covers over his head, wanting to block out the light filtering through the cheap curtains and go back to sleep.

Then again, his colleagues were expecting him. They were due on the road in an hour.

He dragged himself out of bed; a quick glance at the screen of his mobile phone told him that Jane still hadn't replied. And it must be lunchtime in England.

Great.

Just great.

There was no getting away from it: he was going to have to call her if he wanted to find out how she was.

Not now. He needed coffee. He'd call this afternoon.

He showered, feeling like death warmed up, dragged on his clothes and stumbled out into the motel's restaurant. Even the sugar rush of pancakes with way too much maple syrup didn't help much. It took him two minutes to pack. Ten more to check out and throw his things in the back of the van. And then—he had no idea why—he checked his phone again, just before he opened the file he was analysing *en route* to the next rendezvous point.

He stared at the screen in disbelief.

A new text message?

When?

He hadn't heard the phone beep. How the hell could he have missed it? He grimaced. It must've happened while he was in the shower or something.

He flicked into the message and read it.

All OK, due 2nd week Jan.

Well, that told him what he needed to know. He could stop panicking.

But she'd also sent him an attachment.

A photograph.

Mitch's vision blurred as he realised what it was, and the hand holding the phone was actually shaking. He'd never seen a scan photograph before. Oh, sure, colleagues had shown him pictures when their wives had become pregnant, but he'd always just smiled politely and made the right noises. He'd deliberately altered his focus so he hadn't been able to see the picture properly—so he hadn't had to face other people having what he'd lost.

This was different.

A picture of the baby.

His baby.

'You OK, Mitch?' Brad asked.

No. 'Yeah. Just didn't sleep well.' Mitch forced a smile to his face and snapped the phone shut before anyone could see what was on the screen. Right now he didn't want any questions. Because he didn't know what the answers were. 'And I have the joy of data analysis all morning,' he added, hoping to distract his colleague.

It worked. 'Better get coffee to go, then.'

'Double espresso. And doughnuts.'

Brad shook his head sadly. 'You need a woman in your life.'

'I've got Harry.'

'She's not a woman. She's *scary*.' Brad laughed. 'And you're not sleeping with her.'

'No.' Mitch made a show of opening the data files.

It was the middle of the afternoon in England. He couldn't really ring Jane until after lunch, his time. And even then he couldn't guarantee that she'd answer his call. After the way he'd acted, he wouldn't blame her for not wanting to talk to him. But he'd make the effort. Today. Lunchtime.

Except at lunchtime they were tracking a storm and he couldn't break off in the middle of things—and then it was too late to call, because she'd be asleep and it wasn't fair to wake her. Sure, he could text—but then what could he say?

He'd call her tomorrow.

Another sleepless night. A night where he knew he was being a complete and utter bastard for not replying to Jane's text; yet he couldn't think how to reply, either. What to say. How could you want something and yet not want it at the same time?

A baby.

Their baby.

But if he let himself get close to her, if he took the risk—what if he lost her? What if his nightmare turned out to be a recurrent one? What if, in three weeks' time, he got another phone call telling him news that would shatter the life he'd tried so hard to build?

He buried himself in work so he didn't have to think about it. Thank God his wasn't a nine-to-five job—and that this project demanded weekend work, too.

By the end of the next day, his head hurt, and he still hadn't called Jane. Even as he called himself all sorts of coward, he couldn't make himself do the right thing and call her.

Running scared.

Another bad night and a day that dragged. And another.

And then he pressed the wrong button and deleted a whole morning's work on the laptop. Work he couldn't get back because he hadn't been careful enough to save a backup of the file and he'd overwritten it.

Kicking the tyres of the pick-up did nothing to ease his frustration. All it did was give him a sore toe.

'Right.' Brad shoved a bag of doughnuts into his hand, and pushed a cup of coffee into his other hand. 'Sit.'

'What?'

'Now, I know you don't like talking. You Englishmen and your stiff upper lip. But something's been bugging you ever since you came back from England. You haven't been yourself.

So either you need to talk to someone about it, or you need to go and sort it out.'

Mitch took a swig of coffee. 'Thanks. This is good stuff.'

'And don't try to avoid the subject. You don't normally go around kicking the pick-up. So what did you just do?'

Mitch blew out a breath. 'Screwed up a whole morning's data.'

Brad shrugged. 'Then switch to the backup. You've only lost a couple of hours.'

'I didn't make a backup. And I overwrote the wrong file.'

'Oh, what?' Brad stared at him. 'That's definitely not like you. Look, you might be this project leader, but until you sort out whatever's bugging you, you're a liability. Yesterday you misread the weather system and we missed the tornado. The day before you had your camera on the wrong F-stop and your pictures were a mess. Today you've screwed up the data. Tomorrow, you could direct us into a core punch.'

'I wouldn't do anything that stupid.' He might get them in the wrong position to see the tornado—but he definitely wouldn't make the team drive through the bands of heavy rain and hail to get to the other side, an incredibly risky technique known as 'punching the core'. 'It's cool, Brad. I just...' The admission nearly choked him. 'I haven't been sleeping well.'

'Talk to her,' Brad advised.

Mitch played dumb. 'To whom?'

'Whoever the woman is on your mind. And don't pretend there isn't one—I've seen the signs too many times before.'

Mitch set his coffee on the bonnet of the pick-up, then opened the bag of doughnuts, offering them to Brad before taking one himself. 'It's complicated.'

'Women always are.'

'I'm behaving like a complete idiot,' Mitch admitted.

'To her or to us?' Brad asked, raising one eyebrow.

'Both,' Mitch said ruefully. 'And trying to pretend nothing's happening...'

'It never works,' Brad told him sagely. 'And once it starts affecting your job, you're sunk.'

'Yeah.' Mitch sighed. It was time he stopped running away and faced up to the situation. 'I'll arrange for someone to take my place for a week. And when I get back, everything'll be sorted.'

Though he had a feeling that would be much easier said than done.

CHAPTER SEVEN

ON FRIDAY evening, Jane left her desk, intending to head for home—but she stopped as she walked into the reception area of the office.

No. She had to be imagining things. Of course the dark-haired guy sitting in the corner wasn't Mitch. He wasn't even in the country.

But then he spotted her. Stood up. Smiled.

And as he walked towards her her treacherous heart turned over, like a puppy desperate to have its tummy rubbed.

'Hello, Jane.'

'What are you doing here?' she demanded.

He lifted one shoulder in that sexy half-shrug she remembered. 'I've come to see you.'

He'd sent her those texts, wanting to know if everything was all right. And then silence again, when she'd sent him the scan photo. So why on earth was he here now? Or was he just back in the country briefly on business and thought he might amuse himself for the evening? She lifted her chin and stared at him. 'Why?'

'Because…' He sighed. 'I owe you an apology.' He brought his hands from behind his back and handed her the most beautiful bouquet of summery flowers. Not so huge that he was just being a show-off—but not a small bunch just grabbed from the nearest flower stall or supermarket, either. The perfect bouquet.

She blinked away the prickle of tears. Wretched hormones. 'Thank you.' But it still didn't mean he was forgiven. She hated the way he'd blown hot and cold on her—how she never knew what to expect from him. She didn't want dull and predictable; but she didn't want all this uncertainty, either. She wanted somewhere in the middle ground. Someone who was reliable but exciting, too.

'Can I take you to dinner?'

What? He'd given her the silent treatment, hadn't replied to her text, didn't want anything to do with the baby they'd made—and he thought he could just breeze back into her life and ask her to dinner, and a bunch of flowers would make everything all right?

She was about to tell him where to go—and what to do with his flowers, for good measure—when she noticed the deep shadows under his eyes.

He was clearly sleeping as badly as she was, right now.

So maybe he really meant this apology.

And maybe if they went to dinner he'd talk to her. Explain just what was going on in his head—because it was a complete mystery to her.

'Please?' he added softly.

She dragged in a breath. 'OK. I'll have dinner with you. But I need to ring the girls first and tell them I'll be late home.'

'Your housemates.'

She nodded. 'Because I don't want them worrying about me.' Just in case he didn't get the message, she placed her hand over her abdomen. She wasn't showing yet, but she hoped the gesture made the point. They were interested in the baby and cared, whereas the baby's biological father hadn't shown a scrap of interest or caring.

'No need for them to worry. I'll take you home in a taxi.'

Nobody was home, so she left a message saying she was going out to dinner with a friend—she knew that being more specific would probably result in a barrage of phone calls and texts telling her she was crazy and offering to come and rescue her—and that she would get a taxi home.

When they'd found a restaurant, ordered drinks and sat down, Mitch noticed the slightly anxious expression on Jane's face as she looked at the menu. 'What's the matter?' he asked.

'Do you think they'll, um, cook me something a bit plainer, if I ask?'

She'd enjoyed the rich food they'd eaten before; it was odd that she wanted plain food now. But fine, he'd go with the flow. He didn't want a fight over something so trivial. 'Sure. I'll ask for you.'

'Thanks. I'm just not very good with strong smells at the moment.'

'Why not?'

She closed the menu. 'Morning sickness. Strong smells make me feel a bit queasy.'

Oh, hell. Back to the baby again. He really didn't want to talk about the baby—even though that was why he was here. He wasn't ready. Food was a nice, neutral topic—he switched back to what they'd been talking about. 'What do you want to eat, then?'

'Grilled chicken, plain boiled rice, steamed veg—that sort of thing.'

'Sure.' When the waiter came over to take their order, Mitch explained what Jane wanted, and ordered a jug of iced water to go with their meal. He also made sure his own food wasn't something that would smell too strong.

And although the food was good, conversation was awkward—and Jane kept disappearing.

At the fourth time, Mitch leaned back in his chair and looked her straight in the eye. 'Are you trying to avoid me?'

'What makes you think that?' She frowned, looking puzzled.

'You keep making an excuse to go to the loo,' he pointed out.

'It's not an excuse. It's the effect of hormones—I'm either feeling sick or needing to pee. A lot.' She grimaced. 'And I fall asleep at the drop of a hat.'

'Oh.' He felt the colour shoot into his face. Stupid. He ought to know.

Then again, he'd never had anything to do with babies. And as for the dark days of two years ago... Well, it hadn't reached this stage. He'd had no reason to read up on it. And he tended to avoid any book title with the p-word or the b-word anyway.

'Sorry,' he muttered. 'And actually, that's what I wanted to do. Apologise for the way I treated you. Before. When you told me.' He still couldn't bring himself to say the word. *Baby.*

'So why did you?'

'I...' He knew he should tell her—that he owed her a proper explanation—but the words stuck to the roof of his mouth and refused to come out. 'It was a bit of a shock,' he prevaricated. It was the truth. Just not the whole truth.

'It was a shock to me, too.'

'I'm sorry,' he repeated.

'So what does this mean? That you want to be involved after all?'

'I...' He hadn't expected this. He blew out a breath. 'Let's just take this slowly.'

She shook her head, her mouth thinning. 'You're unbelievable.'

Ah, hell. He didn't want her to walk out on him. But at the same time he couldn't tell her the things he'd kept locked inside for so long. He reached across the table and took her hand. 'This isn't an easy situation, Jane. For either of us.'

'Right. So now you've got that off your chest, you're going to disappear again.'

It was a statement, not a question. 'No. Well, not *immediately*,' he admitted.

'When are you going?'

'In about a week.'

'I see.'

He rubbed the pad of his thumb across the backs of her fingers. 'I'm here for a few days, Jane. Why don't we spend the time together? Get to know each other better?'

'Because I have a job. I can't just take time off at your whim.'

'I don't mean during the day. I have things to do here.' Nothing he couldn't do from a distance or leave to Harry, but that wasn't the point. 'Look, tomorrow's Saturday. We can spend the day together. Go out somewhere. You choose where you want to go.'

'You honestly think I want to spend the day with you?'

'We had a good time before,' he reminded her. 'Walking round, seeing the sights, having tea at the Ritz.' *Having sex.* Not that this was the right time to remind her of that. She was clearly still angry with him.

Though there was also still that spark between them. The feeling that made his blood heat. And he could see in her eyes that it was the same for her, too—even though she was clearly trying to resist it.

'I'll think about it.'

He wasn't going to beg. But he did his best to be charming, amusing company until the end of dinner. Until she started yawning—hadn't she said that she fell asleep at the drop of a hat at the moment?

'I'll take you home,' he said. He called a cab and settled the bill while they were waiting. When the taxi pulled up outside her house in Old Isleworth, he kissed her cheek. 'See you tomorrow, then. Ten o'clock.'

'I...' She sighed. 'OK. Ten o'clock.'

'Good.' He made the taxi wait until Jane was safely inside and had closed the front door, and then headed back to the short-let flat Harry had organised for him.

He actually slept properly, that night. And the next morning he rang Jane's doorbell at precisely ten.

To his relief, she was the one who answered it rather than any of her housemates. He wasn't in the mood for any of her friends having a go at him.

'Ready?' he asked.

'Ready.' Her eyes widened as he shepherded her to the car and opened the passenger door for her. 'I thought you said you lived out of a suitcase?'

'I do. This is a hire car.' He shrugged. 'It's easier than sorting out garaging and what have you while I'm out of the country.'

'But it's a soft top. And low-slung. And…'

'Extravagant. Yes, I know. It's still a lot cheaper to hire it than to buy one and deal with all the administrative hassles and maintenance and stuff.' He waved a dismissive hand. 'Hop in. So where do you fancy going?'

'How about Hampton Court?' she suggested. 'It's a nice day, and the gardens are really pretty.'

'Sure.' He smiled at her. 'You've been before?'

She nodded. 'Not for a while, though. And I haven't found my way through the maze.'

'I'm good at navigation.'

'You think you can do the maze?'

He shrugged. 'It's a mathematical puzzle. I work with numbers all the time. It shouldn't be a problem.'

'No way.'

'Is that a challenge?' He raised an eyebrow. 'Right. If I do it, you buy me a cream tea.'

'And if you don't?'

'Then you can choose a forfeit.'

Their eyes met, and he really hoped that the forfeit she was thinking of was the same one in his mind.

And then she smiled. 'Deal.'

He drove them out to East Moseley and they spent the day

wandering through the state rooms and Tudor kitchens at Hampton Court. There were some old documents on display in one of the exhibitions, and Mitch noticed how Jane's eyes lit up.

'Can you actually read that?' he asked, staring at the illegible squiggles.

She raised an eyebrow, then read the first couple of paragraphs out loud to him without so much as a stumble, as if she were reading capitals on a ten-foot-high poster.

'That's impressive,' he said.

'It's practice. I'm used to the style of handwriting and the kind of abbreviations they use. So I know that squiggle there above the G—' she pointed it out to him '—means the clerk missed out the I and the N before it. Just as you could look at a weather map and tell me exactly what was going on, whereas to me it would look like random blobs and lines.'

'You love that stuff, don't you?'

She nodded. 'It's a window into another world.'

Mitch found himself holding her hand while they walked through the gardens. And her fingers were curled just as tightly round his as his were around hers.

When they'd reached the centre of the maze and came out again, he breathed on the nails of his free hand and polished them on his T-shirt. 'I believe you disputed my navigational skills. So you owe me a cream tea, Ms Redmond.'

She rolled her eyes. 'Do you ever stop thinking about food?'

He leaned over to whisper in her ear. 'Yes. I have a two-track mind.'

She blushed beautifully, and he grinned at her. He laughed even more when she cuffed his arm. But when they finally returned to the car, he realised how much he'd enjoyed the day. How much he'd enjoyed just being with her.

Dangerously so.

He knew he should drive her home and spend the evening working on the data Brad had emailed to him. And yet he found himself suggesting having dinner that evening at a small pub. And from there somehow they ended up back at his place. Just sitting quietly on the sofa together, listening to music—and she fell asleep in his arms.

'Hey, sleepyhead,' he said, gently waking her.

'Huh?' She yawned and blinked. 'Sorry. Better call a taxi.'

He'd had a couple of glasses of wine with his meal, so he couldn't drive her home. And besides, he didn't want today to end. 'Why don't you stay here?'

'Because you've only got one bed. And we're sitting on it.'

But he had a feeling that her protest was half-hearted, because she hadn't moved out of the warmth of his arms. He kissed the top of her head. 'By the time you've called your housemates and cleaned your teeth—and I just so happen to have a spare toothbrush still in its box—I'll have this made up.' He held her just a little bit more tightly. 'Stay with me tonight.'

She tensed for a moment, and he guessed what was worrying her. 'I'm not going to pounce on you.' Even though he wanted to. 'You're tired. You need some sleep. Better to go to bed now, than go home in a taxi and end up with a crick in your neck from falling asleep at an awkward angle.'

Put that way, it made sense. Jane relaxed. 'OK. Thank you.'

And by the time she'd called Hannah to explain she was really tired so she was staying overnight, Mitch had found her a toothbrush—as promised, still in its box—and left her a pile of towels and his robe.

When she'd finished in the bathroom, he'd made the bed. And when she slid under the covers beside him, still wearing his robe, she felt self-conscious. Couldn't relax. She wriggled further down the bed, but she just felt too awkward to get comfortable. Curled away from him felt wrong. Curled towards him felt needy. In the end she lay on her back—and that wasn't comfortable, either.

He leaned over and kissed the tip of her nose. 'You're all tense. And I happen to know a pretty good way of relaxing.'

Sex?

She must have spoken the word aloud, because he laughed. 'Contrary to popular belief, most men don't have a one-track mind.'

'Don't they?'

'No. And I said I wouldn't pounce on you.' He brushed his mouth lightly against hers, then whispered, 'Take that robe off and turn over. Onto your front. And close your eyes.'

And then he was stroking her back. Gliding his hands all the way up to her neck, then feathering them down her sides. Slow and easy. A rhythm that melted away all the knots in her back and made her feel as if she were floating on a cloud.

'Like it?' His lips brushed her earlobe.

'Mmm.' The noise came out practically as a purr, and he laughed softly.

'Told you so.'

'You have amazing…' She couldn't open her eyes any more. Or her mouth. She just slid into blissful sleep.

Mitch switched off the light, turned onto his side and pulled Jane into the curve of his body.

But it was a long time before he slept.

Right now he had the closeness, the intimacy he'd missed so much since Natalie. And it scared him stupid.

How could you want something so much and yet not want it at the same time? he wondered. It would be so easy to fall in love with Jane. She made him smile, she fenced intellectually with him and she could arouse him with a single glance. She was his opposite in many ways—and yet he liked that.

But if he let himself love her…supposing it all went wrong again? The chances were, he wouldn't lose her the way he'd lost

Natalie. But there was another problem. He was never in one place too long—his job took him away a lot. And she was settled here—too settled to want to move. Although their differences made things interesting, maybe in the end they would be too much for a relationship to survive.

And he didn't think his heart would survive the shredding.

Tomorrow, he'd work out how to tell her that they should maybe cool this off. He'd support her and the baby financially, but he couldn't give her more.

But tonight he'd just enjoy her being in his arms.

Jane woke the next morning, warm and comfortable with a body spooned round hers. A very male body. Mitch had one arm wrapped round her ribcage, and his fingers were curved round her breast.

'Just relax and go back to sleep,' a voice murmured drowsily in her ear. 'I'm comfortable.'

'I need the loo.'

'What, again?' He groaned, but released her so she could go to the bathroom. And the second she returned to bed, he pulled her close again. 'Go back to sleep,' he muttered.

But she couldn't.

Not when he was touching her like this.

'Mitch?'

'What now?' He sounded resigned rather than grumpy. Good.

She wriggled slightly. 'Do you know where your left hand is?'

'Uh-huh. And it's very comfortable where it is. *Go to sleep.*'

How could she? She was too aware of him—of his clean male scent, of the warmth of his body. And of his erection pressed very firmly against her back. She wriggled again.

'You're *such* a fidget,' he protested.

'I'm *awake.*'

'You're a morning person?'

'Yes.' She sighed. 'Don't tell me you're a night owl.'

She felt his mouth against her shoulder. 'No. I burn the candle at both ends, honey.'

Oh, God. The pictures *that* roused in her mind.

She shifted again, and he pulled her closer. 'I wouldn't wriggle about too much if I were you.'

'Why?'

'Because…' He tilted his hips slightly, pushing his erection against her. 'That's why.'

'Oh-h-h.' She felt her face flame.

'Go back to sleep. I'm tired. You kept me awake all last night, snoring.'

'I do *not* snore,' she said huffily. At least, she was pretty sure she didn't.

'I was teasing.' His mouth drifted along her skin again. 'Mmm. You smell nice.' Another kiss, and this time his thumb moved to stroke her nipple; the friction between the pad of his thumb and her skin made her shiver.

'You're wriggling again, Janey.' There was definite amusement in his voice—along with something much, much headier.

Arousal.

'Mmm.' He smoothed his hand over the undercurve of her breast, down over her abdomen; then his fingers hooked over the edge of her knickers. 'These are in the way of what I really, really want to do right now.'

She shivered. 'Mitch.'

'You feel nice,' he said softly. 'You smell nice. And right now there's nothing I want to do more than to make love with you.'

Her breath hitched. He hadn't said 'have sex'. He'd said 'make love'. With her, not to her. What he had in mind was clearly very much mutual.

'Janey.' He tilted his hips again.

'I… I don't know what to say.'

'"Yes" would do,' he said, and nuzzled her shoulder again.

'I…' She tipped her head back, then wriggled round so she was lying on her back. 'Yes.'

Her smile could have melted snow—and it made his blood sizzle.

Mitch temporarily lost it. He had no idea who actually finished removing her knickers, and he didn't care—because then they were skin to skin, just the way he'd ached to be, and he was kneeling between her thighs. She was kissing him back, stroking him, teasing him to the point where he was going to implode.

And then she moved slightly, so the tip of his penis nudged against her entrance. Like warm, wet silk sheathing him.

His resistance went completely and he tilted his hips. Thrust slow and easy and blissfully deep.

'That's good,' she whispered.

'Yeah. You feel incredible,' he whispered back. 'The perfect fit.'

And then it hit him. They weren't using a condom.

Considering the situation, it would've been like closing the proverbial stable door.

But even so—they really shouldn't be doing this. He was supposed to be cooling things down.

And then he stopped thinking at all as her muscles tightened round him. All he could do was keep pushing deep inside her. Watch the way her pupils expanded, her breathing grew shallow, and then suddenly she was there, at the peak, her body tightening round his.

She called out his name, her voice all shuddery, and he jammed his mouth over hers, not wanting the moment to end. The moment when his climax hit him and pushed him over the edge, right along with her.

He wasn't sure how long they lay there together afterwards. Fulfilled. Warm. At peace.

But finally she stirred. 'I should go home.'

'It's Sunday. Do you have to be anywhere?'

'No-o.'

'Then spend today with me. I promise I'll take you home safely tonight.' He wasn't quite sure why he was saying this but right now he didn't want to move. He was comfortable with Jane in his arms, her head pillowed on his shoulder and her arm wrapped round his waist.

'Mitch. I need a shower.'

He dropped a kiss on her hair. 'Want me to join you and wash your back?'

'I…look, we can't stay in bed all day.'

He didn't see why not, but he sighed. 'All right. I'll make us some breakfast.'

He didn't bother to dress, just climbed out of bed; Jane headed for the bathroom. He'd switched on the kettle and taken fruit from the fridge when he heard the unmistakable sound of retching.

'Jane? Are you OK?' he called.

'Morning sickness,' she mumbled. 'I thought it meant feeling sick, not…'

And she was promptly sick again.

He took a bottle of water from the fridge and poured a glass for her, then rapped on the bathroom door and walked in. He put the glass down on the window sill, then ran warm water into the sink, soaked a flannel and wrung it out.

'It's OK,' he said softly, wiping her face.

'I feel horrible,' she said, her face white.

And he'd left her to deal with this on her own.

Just as he'd left Natalie.

Well, he hadn't known about Natalie's pregnancy when he'd gone to the Antarctic. But he knew about Jane's. And it made him feel like pondlife. How could he just walk away from this and let her deal with it alone? What sort of man was he?

Ha. He already knew that. A coward.

One who was too scared to stay in case his heart got involved again.

He wiped her face. 'Sip this water,' he said, lifting the glass to her mouth. 'Slowly. What do you normally eat when you feel like this?'

'Dry crackers.'

'I haven't got any. The best I can do is dry toast.'

She shook her head. 'I can't face that. Toast *smells*.'

He stroked her hair. 'Does this happen a lot?'

'It's the first time I've actually been sick. And I thought it was supposed to stop being this bad by now.' She grimaced.

He stroked her face. 'Just help yourself to whatever you need. And if you want me to do anything, just yell, OK? I'll get your clothes and leave them outside the bathroom door.'

'Thanks.' She smiled wanly at him and continued sipping water.

By the time she emerged from the bathroom, fully dressed, he'd sorted out the sofa bed and tidied up. 'Can I get you some toast now?'

'No.' She shuddered. 'But thanks for the offer.'

'Coffee?'

'Just water. Thanks.'

He remembered she couldn't handle smells. So he asked first. 'Do you mind if I have coffee?'

Her sudden pallor told him the answer. She'd be brave about it if he pushed, but he wasn't going to be that self-centred and put his own need for coffee above hers for avoiding smells that made her ill. 'OK. I'll stick to juice,' he said, and headed for the fridge.

CHAPTER EIGHT

AFTER breakfast, Mitch took Jane back to her house so she could change, and it drove her crazy that he refused to come in and meet her housemates. She didn't quite believe his excuse that he had some emails he needed to answer so he'd work in the car while she was getting ready—she knew it would still be well before the crack of dawn in America right then—but at the same time she didn't want to push him and break the new harmony between them.

And she was glad she hadn't when he drove her back to the centre of London.

'I thought we'd have a chill-out day,' Mitch said, parking in a little back street she'd never seen before.

But as soon as they walked to the main road she knew exactly where she was. 'St James's Park.'

'The perfect walk on a perfect summer's day,' he said.

Blue skies, sunshine, and warm without being sticky or humid. Mitch's fingers curled round hers and they walked over by the water, watching the flamingoes and the pelicans that lived on Duck Island.

He was almost right, she thought. Except he'd missed a word out. It was the perfect *romantic* summer's day. Especially when, every so often, he spun her round to face him and stole a kiss. Or gave her one of those smiles that sent her knees weak.

This was the man she'd fallen for on her birthday—not the cold, aloof stranger he'd become the next time she'd seen him.

They had lunch in a little tapas bar; Mitch didn't ask her what she wanted, but ordered a huge array of dishes and some plain bread to mop everything up. And because they were eating outside on a little terrace in the shade of a parasol, the spicier scents were blown away by the light breeze and she could eat without feeling queasy.

When she couldn't decide what to try first, Mitch smiled at her. 'Close your eyes and open your mouth.'

'What?'

'Just do it.' He wrinkled his nose to take the edge off the command.

She closed her eyes. And then she felt him brush something along her lower lip, tempting her to take the morsel from his fingers. One of the salty, glossy black olives she'd liked the look of.

It was a game she'd never played before—and she was surprised by how arousing she found it. Even more so when she opened her eyes and kept her gaze fixed on his as he fed her. Because they were in the shade, they'd both pushed their sunglasses on top of their heads—and those beautiful grey-green eyes were hot. This was turning him on, too.

Well, what was sauce for the goose…

She took a cube of the marinated halloumi cheese. 'Close your eyes,' she said.

She could see the spark of amusement in his gaze, but he did as she asked. And when he ate the morsel she fed him, she could feel the warmth of his mouth against her finger and thumb. That was a deliberate pout, she was sure, so he could kiss her fingertips.

Talk about sexy.

If they weren't in a public place…

Then he opened his eyes. And his gaze was smouldering.

Sultry. Telling her that he was thinking exactly the same as she was.

She rubbed an olive against his lower lip—and then licked her own lip.

He dragged in a breath. 'Jane, are you trying to vamp me?'

Yup. And she thought it was working. But she spread her hands and pretended demureness. 'What, on a crowded terrace in the middle of the afternoon?'

He leaned closer, as if to whisper in her ear, and she could feel the warmth of his breath against her neck. His lips were a few millimetres from her skin. And it shocked her how much she wanted him to kiss her.

She felt his teeth graze her earlobe—not hard enough to hurt, but enough to tell her that he wanted her. Right here. Right now.

'It's working,' he whispered.

After that, lunch didn't last long.

And Mitch was lucky not to get a speeding fine on the way back to his flat.

She'd also never seen a sofa bed opened so quickly. And just as well. She couldn't wait any more, either. Couldn't spin out the pleasure of undressing him—she wanted him right here, right now. She didn't care that it was the middle of the afternoon. She didn't care that the curtains weren't drawn, either; they were on the top floor and the muslin net at the windows was thick enough that nobody would see them. Though at the same time it was thin enough that the warm summer light flooded the room and hid nothing.

He had beautiful shoulders. Beautiful arms, too; she could feel the muscles, like thick ropes, telling her how strong he was.

Strong enough to pick her up—as if he were carrying her over the threshold—and carry her to the bed.

With every touch, every brush of his lips against her body, he was stoking her temperature higher and higher. Exploring. Teasing. Tasting. When his mouth closed around one nipple and sucked, hard, the shiver of pleasure slid all the way down her body, and she pushed her fingers into his hair, urging him on.

When he traced a lazy path down her midriff with the tip of his tongue, she was practically hyperventilating. And when he parted her thighs and she felt his breath warm against her sex, every nerve in her body tingled.

She could have screamed in frustration when, instead of stroking his tongue right along the spot where she needed it most, he kissed his way down her thigh to the back of her knee.

'If you tease me much longer, I'm going to…' Her breath hitched.

'Is that meant to be a threat?' He moved across to the other knee, caressing the sensitive spot in a way that aroused her but made her want so much more.

'N-no.' What was wrong with her? Why couldn't she get the words out? 'I…' OK. One at a time, with deep breaths in between. 'Want. You. To.' Her whole body quivered.

'Touch you?' he guessed. 'Here?'

The lightest caress over her clitoris. Right where she wanted to be touched—but the pressure was too light to be anything more than teasing.

'M-more.' Her voice was shaking, and she pushed herself harder against his hand.

He slid one finger into her. 'Better?'

'No.'

He added a second finger. 'How about now?'

'N-no. Stop.'

He removed his hand. 'OK.'

'No!' She opened her eyes and glared at him.

'"Stop" usually means "no",' he reminded her.

'I was trying to say,' she told him through gritted teeth, 'stop *teasing* me.'

His gaze went hot. 'Then why don't you tell me what you want?'

She felt the colour shoot into her face. 'I…'

'Shy?'

That did it. She sat up and pushed him onto the bed. 'Better than telling. I'll show you.'

'I love it when you go bossy on me.'

He'd be laughing on the other side of his face in a minute, she vowed. Because she'd tease him just the way he'd teased her. Drive him to the point of begging. She kissed her way down his body, and was rewarded by a shudder.

Good.

She hadn't finished, yet. Not by a long way.

She drew a circle round his navel with the tip of her tongue. Followed the arrowing of hair downwards—and swerved just before she reached the tip of his penis.

He sucked in a breath. 'Jane. You're…'

Ha. Right where she wanted him. Just this side of incoherent. She breathed along his erection, and even though his hands tangled in her hair and his breath came in little shuddering gasps, begging her to go that bit further, she kept that tiny, all-important distance.

'Jane.' He dragged in a breath. 'I'm…going…to…'

'Is that meant to be a threat?' She tossed his words back at him.

'No. Begging. Janey. *Please.*'

She straddled him. Took him in one hand. And slowly, slowly eased herself onto him. Millimetre by millimetre. Watching the expression on his face, all the while; seeing desire mingle with pleasure and wonder and delight.

'Oh, yes.' His voice had dropped an octave and the words sounded as if they came through sandpaper. 'Do you have any idea how good you feel—?'

He stopped speaking as she began to move. And he laced his fingers through hers, pushing up as she pushed down, his eyes intense as he looked at her.

She knew the exact moment he lost control.

Because it was the same for her, too.

And when the peak hit them both, he sat up, wrapped his arms round her and kissed her as if he were drowning and she were his last breath of oxygen.

They didn't get out of bed for the rest of the day. Except for Mitch to grab his mobile phone and order a Chinese take-away. Which they ate in bed, too.

She was warm and comfortable just lying there in his arms, listening to a classical music station on the radio. But tomorrow was Monday and life had to go back to normal.

Regretfully, she pressed a kiss onto his chest and sat up. 'I really should go home.'

'Why?'

'I have work tomorrow. And I assume you do too.'

'Mmm.' He stroked her hair. 'Any chance you can get some time off, this week? Even if it's just a day?'

'I'll talk to my boss. It depends on who else is off.'

'Uh-huh. You know, you could go to work from here tomorrow,' he suggested, clearly as unwilling for her to leave as she was.

'I haven't got my office clothes here. Or clean underwear. Or…'

He sat up too and held her close. 'OK. I'll meet you from work tomorrow, then. We can go to the cinema, then for a meal somewhere.'

'That'd mean a late night.' She shook her head. 'I can't do late nights when I have to get up for work the next morning.'

He dropped a kiss on the top of her head. 'This is nearer the West End than your place is—so if you stayed here tomorrow night, it wouldn't mean a late night for you. When I run you home, you can pack an overnight bag and give it to me to bring back here for tomorrow.'

'I…'

He rubbed his hand along the top of her arm. 'How about if I let you choose the film?'

'You'd sit through a chick-flick?' she challenged. That was *so* not his type of thing. He'd go for an action movie, she was sure.

'Given enough ice cream, and the fact I'll be spending the night with you afterwards—yep, I think I can sit through a chick-flick.' He sounded amused.

'OK. And you'll come in and meet my housemates tonight?'

'When I've taken you home, I have work to do.'

Yet again he'd backed away from being part of her life.

This really wasn't going to work.

Her tension must have communicated itself to him, because he nuzzled her cheek. 'Jane. Stop worrying. Everything's going to be just fine.'

Over the next couple of days, Jane began to feel as if their relationship was becoming real. Becoming stronger. Mitch met her from work the following evening, as they'd arranged, and, even though she could tell he was bored to tears and he barely laughed once, he sat through the romantic comedy she'd chosen without moaning.

'You hated it, didn't you?' she asked when they'd ordered their meal.

He gave her a slow, sexy smile. 'Yes. But you know what they say—no pain, no gain.'

'That's aerobics.'

His smile grew positively wicked. 'Exactly.'

Though their lovemaking that night wasn't energetic and exhausting. It was slow and gentle and so tender that it made her want to cry. Because this felt like more than just sex. It felt like a declaration of love.

On Tuesday night, Mitch met her from work; again, they had dinner out, and had a stroll by the river, but he took her back home in a taxi and made sure she was indoors safely before he let the taxi drive off again.

He hadn't spoken once about the baby since that first evening back. Then again, this time round he'd said he wanted to take it slowly. Maybe he just needed time with her to get used to the idea. Maybe he was coming round—realising that he was going to be a father.

The tiniest flicker of hope lit her from within. And maybe, just maybe, this was going to work out

On Wednesday—seeing as she'd managed to get the day off—he actually came over to her place.

'You're scared of them, aren't you?' Jane teased as she answered the door to him.

'Who?'

'My housemates. You've been waiting until they're at work before you came over. Supposing one of them was off sick or had changed shifts?'

'Be still, my quaking knees,' he said with a grin. 'I'm not scared of them at all. It's just my time's limited and I want to spend it with *you*.'

But he let her show him round and made all the right noises. Until he saw her room.

'It's the furthest from the bathroom.'

She shrugged. 'It's fine.'

'No, it isn't,' he said. 'You're up and down at night like a yo-yo.'

She flapped a dismissive hand. 'That'll pass.'

'And it's tiny. It's not a room, it's a shoebox.'

'I *like* my room,' she said defensively.

'It's very nice,' he said, clearly trying to placate her. 'But it's tiny. And that bed…it's not even a full-width single bed.'

'It's *fine*.'

'It's the sort of bed a student would have.'

She shrugged. 'I think this used to be a student house.'

'You're not a student any more,' he pointed out.

True. She had a job. And she was going to be a single mother, in a few months' time.

Well, she'd cope. She had her housemates to support her. She'd be fine.

Though his comments about her room cast a bit of a shadow over the day. Why was he making such a fuss about it, when he wasn't even going to be around?

She forced herself to smile when he took her to a modern art gallery.

'What's up?' he asked, giving her a sidelong glance.

'Nothing.'

'You don't like modern art?'

'I'm a bit more traditional,' she admitted. Put her in the British Library among the illuminated manuscripts and Books of Hours, and she was in heaven. Cubism and abstracts just didn't speak to her in the same way.

'I know it's not everyone's cup of tea. Though bear with me here as there's one thing I wanted to show you—it's amazing.' He talked her through several other pieces, getting her to view them in a slightly different light when she thought of them in terms of colour and shape and texture.

And then he paused in the doorway. As if he were waiting for her reaction.

She glanced through and saw immediately what he wanted her to see: a huge orangey-yellow disc, backlit. Like a rising sun. And there was something really elemental about it.

'That's *beautiful*.'

'It's chalcedony. It looks fabulous from a distance. But close up it's just as interesting because you can see impurities in the stone that look like sunspots. And the way the light works through the stone…'

Clearly this was something that touched a nerve with him.

She wasn't sure why—but she was glad he'd wanted to share his sense of wonder with her.

She tried to blank the thought as soon as it formed, but it seeped insidiously through into her head. A sense of wonder. Would Mitch ever share her sense of wonder about the baby?

There was no point in asking him because she knew he wouldn't discuss it. But by the end of the day she knew he'd let her a little bit closer. Maybe all he needed was time.

On Thursday, Mitch spent the day doing something he'd never thought he'd do.

Flat-hunting.

For a place where Jane would be much more comfortable—with a king-size bed and an *en suite* bathroom. She couldn't stay where she was now, and as he wasn't going to be around at least he could help her with this.

He started by checking local estate agencies on the Internet. Pages and pages of places that were too small or in the wrong area or didn't have an *en suite* or were perfectly serviceable but—from what he'd seen of the house where she lived now—he didn't think would be to Jane's taste. Seeing as he lived out of a suitcase most of the time, he didn't really care where he lived, but he knew that she did. A lot.

And then he hit gold.

The flat was close to where she lived now and had the right sort of layout. Better still, when he rang the agent to check if it was still going to be available, it turned out that the flat was vacant because previous tenants had just bought their first home; although they'd paid the rent until the end of the month to make sure they weren't left in a mess if the deal fell through, they'd already moved out. If he took the flat this weekend they'd get some money back from the landlord. And he'd be able to get Jane settled in before he left for the States.

Everybody won.

'I'd like to view it,' he said.

'Certainly, sir. When?'

He glanced at his watch. 'I'll be at your office in an hour. Sooner if I can make it through the traffic.'

And when he saw it, he knew it was the right place. Clean and well maintained. Ground floor, so she wouldn't have to struggle with stairs. The previous tenants had been there for two years, so he could be confident that the neighbours were fine—if they weren't, there would've been a much higher turnover of tenancies. No signs of damp. And, best of all, it was furnished: with a king-sized bed.

She'd be comfortable.

And near a bathroom.

'Let's go back to your office so I can look over the tenancy agreement.'

'You want to take it?' the estate agent asked, looking hopeful.

'I think so. If I do take it, can I have the keys this afternoon?'

He met Jane from work as usual. Greeted her with a kiss. Took her out for dinner. And then gave the taxi driver the address very quietly, out of Jane's earshot.

'Why have we stopped here?' Jane asked when the taxi pulled up.

'There's something I want you to see.'

She frowned. 'Such as?'

'Patience is a virtue,' he intoned.

She cuffed him. 'Not one you possess, so don't give me that.'

He laughed, and opened the front door.

Her frown deepened. 'Mitch? What's going on?'

'Have a look round.'

She walked from room to room. 'It's a flat. An empty one.'

'A furnished one,' he corrected. 'Do you like it?'

'It's OK. Why?'

'Because you're moving in this weekend.'

'I'm *what*?' She stared at him in horror.

'I said, you're moving in this weekend. It's our flat,' he added, just in case she hadn't got the message.

'Our flat?' she repeated.

'Uh-huh. And we're moving your stuff on Saturday.'

'I can't just tell the girls I'm moving out without any notice!'

'Well, of course not.' He'd already thought of that. 'Give them whatever notice you need. I'm paying the rent here anyway.'

'*You're* paying the rent.'

'Obviously.' He'd told her he'd support her financially. This counted as part of that.

'And you're going to live here?'

'When I'm in the country, yes.'

She stared at him and folded her arms. 'You did this without even asking me if I wanted to live with you?'

'It makes sense, Jane. Your bed's tiny and it's not comfortable and it's way too far from the bathroom. Here, you have a king-size bed and an *en suite*. And it's just round the corner from your friends, so you're not going to feel cut off. It's nearer the train station, too, so you won't have to walk so far.'

'Exercise is good for you.'

'And on days when your back's aching?' he pointed out.

She gritted her teeth. 'You could have asked me first. What do you think I am, some little doormat who'll just go along with what you want?'

'No.' He raked a hand through his hair. This wasn't going the way he'd expected. 'You're being difficult about this, Jane. All I've done is try to do something nice for you. Give you more space, and make you more comfortable without cutting you off from everyone.'

'I don't like surprises.'

'You're being unreasonable.'

'Am I?' She shook her head in seeming exasperation. 'You chose the flat without even consulting me.'

'You were at work.'

'You still could've asked me.'

He sighed. 'All right. Let's play fantasy flat. What would your ideal location be? Somewhere near your friends, yes?'

'Yes.'

'And you'd want somewhere with a decent-sized bedroom. Preferably an *en suite*.'

'Well—yes.'

'And with a decent kitchen.'

'Yes.'

His point exactly. 'I've just described this flat. So what's the problem?'

'You didn't ask me first.'

He rolled his eyes. 'Jane. I thought you told me your house-mates called you "Jane-Jane-Superbrain"? And that you're known for being sensible?'

'They do. And I am.'

'This is the sensible option.'

'But you didn't ask me first.'

He folded his arms. 'So you're telling me you'd rather sleep in a tiny bed in a tiny room as far from the bathroom as you can get?'

'No-o.'

'Then what's the problem?'

'How many times do I have to repeat myself? You didn't ask me!'

It had to be hormones making her react this way.

Not that he wanted to think about the reason for those hormones.

'All right. We'll do it your way. Will you move in with me, Jane?'

'We hardly know each other.'

She was supposed to say yes. He bit back a sigh of impatience. 'Isn't this a good way to get to know each other?'

She bit her lip. 'You've got an argument for everything.'

'Most things,' he agreed.

'I hate you.'

'No, you don't.' And he could prove that to her very quickly. It definitely wasn't hate that heated the air between them.

'For all I know, you're really messy and you leave the top off the toothpaste and—'

'Jane,' he cut in softly. 'I live out of a suitcase. I'm tidy.'

'You work with chaos,' she pointed out.

'Which doesn't mean I live in it. I'm house-trained. I can cook.'

She scowled. 'And how am I supposed to know that?'

'My mum's a domestic science teacher, so she'd never hear the end of it if her kids couldn't so much as boil an egg.'

'But we always eat out.'

'Because you find cooking smells difficult. But I'll prove it to you on Saturday night. When we've moved your stuff.'

'When we've what?'

Oh, for goodness' sake. Were they going to have to go through all this again? 'When we've moved your stuff,' he said patiently. 'Do I need to hire a van?'

'You're steamrollering me into this.'

'No. I'm trying to make you comfortable.' He paused. 'So do you like the flat, or do you want this to be a very temporary let while I find something else?'

'I like it,' she admitted.

'Good. So there isn't a problem.'

'I…' Her shoulders drooped. 'I didn't think it would be like this. I thought when a man asked you to move in with him, you'd choose a place together.'

'You were at work, this was perfect, and I needed to move fast to secure it. There wasn't time.' He walked over to her and slid his arms round her. 'I just didn't want to think of you not being comfortable when I could do something about it.' He rested his cheek against her hair. 'I wanted it to be a nice surprise. And I was trying to think about it from your point of view.'

She sniffed. 'I don't mean to be an ungrateful cow.'

He held her closer. 'You're not. And I should've asked you properly. It's just I'm used to seeing what needs to be done and doing it—not waiting to check with someone else first.' He nuzzled her earlobe. 'If you really hate it, find somewhere you like and we'll move.' Then he realised that she was shaking. 'Jane? You're not crying, are you?'

'No-o.' But her voice was suspiciously wobbly.

He held her shoulders and leaned back so he could look at her face. Ah, hell. She *was* crying. He wiped away the tears with the pad of his thumb. 'Don't cry. It'll be fine. Make me a list tonight of the things we need and I'll get them tomorrow while you're at work.'

'So I don't even get to choose them?'

He sighed. 'Make it a specific list. Tell me which shop, which colour—whatever.'

'You sound like my boss's teenagers.' She rolled her eyes and drawled, 'Whatever.'

He laughed. 'I'm just not bothered about colour schemes.'

'So I could have everything hot pink if I wanted it?'

The sparkle was back in her eyes; he knew she was teasing. 'With lime, green spots, if you really have to. Look, I'll get the very basics tomorrow, and that'll tide us over for long enough for you to get what you really want. Which will be my bill, OK?'

She lifted her chin. 'I have a good job. I can pay my way.'

'Fine. Enough arguing. I'll walk you home—text me the list, or email it across, and I'll get as much sorted as I can tomorrow.' His mouth came to within millimetres away from hers. 'And we can christen the flat on Saturday night…'

CHAPTER NINE

ON FRIDAY, Mitch bought everything on Jane's list. He dropped the bedlinen and towels into a laundry service so he could pick them up later, stocked the fridge and the kitchen cupboards, then picked up the laundry and made the bed. If Jane really thought he lived in a mess…well, she'd have to eat her words, because the flat was immaculate. And he'd enjoy teasing her into a forfeit. Like sharing a bath with him.

Then he went to meet her from work.

'How was your shopping trip?' she asked.

'Fine. Everything's there. So either I can cook for you tonight, or we can have dinner out.'

'Or you could have dinner at my place.'

'Don't you mean our place?'

'No. I mean where I live now.' She sighed. 'You're going to have to meet my friends, Mitch. They're helping me move my stuff tomorrow.'

'No need. I can handle it.'

'They look out for me. No way are they going to let me move into a flat without checking things out for themselves.'

Including him, he thought wryly—she didn't mean just the flat. 'All right. Let's compromise. We'll drop by our flat and see if you're happy with it, then I'll come and meet your friends and we'll get a take-away or something.'

She went tearful on him again when she saw the flat. Especially when she read the card on the bouquet of flowers he'd left for her in the middle of the bistro table in the kitchen. 'Happy moving-in day?'

'Jane, you can't cry *now*,' he told her. 'Otherwise your friends will think I'm upsetting you and we'll end up having a huge fight.'

'I'm not crying because I'm sad.' She scrubbed the back of her hand across her eyes. 'It's hormones.'

Uh-huh, and he wanted to steer off that subject right now. There was plenty of time to think about that later. 'Let's go and see your friends, then.'

Meeting her housemates wasn't quite as bad as he'd expected. They gave him a thorough grilling, but he'd expected that and didn't take it personally. It just meant they loved Jane and wanted to make sure she was going to be OK. And that he'd treat her right.

When he left, that evening, he had a feeling the jury was still out.

But when they saw the flat, the following day, he finally won their approval. They could see exactly why he'd chosen it and that it was right for Jane.

'So you're going to turn the little room into a nursery, then?' Charlie asked, when they'd finished moving everything.

He shrugged. 'If that's what Jane wants. But it's still early days.'

Charlie's eyebrow rose. 'Fourteen weeks isn't exactly early days. It's when morning sickness just about stops and she's going to start blooming. And it's the best time to plan things and do things, before she's huge and tired.'

'Give us a chance to move in, first,' he said lightly. He didn't want to think about what happened after 'huge and tired'. About what would happen if he gave his heart to someone so tiny and vulnerable, and then something went wrong. 'Seeing as you three gave up your afternoon to help us move Jane's stuff, do you want to stay for dinner?'

'Take-away?' Hannah asked.

'No. I'm cooking Spanish chicken. With brown rice, broccoli and carrots, followed by fresh fruit salad, to make sure Jane gets her five a day.'

Shelley's eyes widened. 'You can cook?'

He shrugged. 'I already told Jane, my mum's a domestic science teacher and it was a matter of pride for her to make sure my sister and I could cook. I'm perfectly competent in the kitchen.'

'Thanks for the offer,' Charlie said, 'but I can't—I've already arranged to go out with Luke. Though I'll take a rain check.'

'Sure.'

Hannah and Shelley exchanged a glance. 'It's tempting—but we ought to let you get settled. Jane looks tired,' Hannah added.

'I'll make sure she rests.'

He did. He wouldn't even let Jane see them to the door. When she protested, he simply picked her up, settled her on the sofa, and told her to stay put because he'd bring her a drink of iced water when he'd seen the girls out.

'Thanks,' Jane said when he brought her the water. 'You know, they liked you.'

'I'm not so sure. Charlie was grilling me again today. A lot,' he pointed out.

She shrugged. 'That's Charlie. I think she just wanted to make sure you weren't going to mess me about.'

As he had before?

But at least Jane didn't say it.

'Now, I know you like rice and broccoli and chicken,' he said, 'but I just want to check before I start cooking. You're OK with peppers, tomatoes, onions and carrots?'

'Fine. As long as the peppers are capsicum, not hot chilli.' She looked rueful. 'And I'm afraid garlic gives me terrible heartburn at the moment, so that might wreck your recipe a bit.'

'Hey, it's not a problem. I want to feed you, not make you

feel rough,' he said. 'And they're capsicum. Oh, and paprika, but I'll keep a light hand.'

Cooking for two brought back memories for him. Natalie had been a hopeless cook, so the kitchen in their house in Cambridge had been his domain. And he'd really enjoyed cooking. Now he was in a kitchen again, he remembered just how much pleasure he found in cooking: it relaxed him. Chopping and stirring and seasoning and tasting.

But Jane wasn't Natalie.

He had no idea whether she could cook or not. They'd never discussed it. It really didn't matter much either way.

But then it hit him.

When he was in the UK, he'd be living here. With Jane. He'd acted so quickly on impulse that he hadn't had time to think about it in that way. He'd have a proper base for the first time in a long, long while.

And he wasn't quite sure how he felt about that. Whether it made him want to go and curl up next to her—or whether it made him want to run like hell.

When Mitch had finished cooking, he called Jane through, then brought their plates over to the little bistro table.

'This is very good,' she said when she'd tasted the first mouthful. 'So you weren't joking about being able to cook, then.'

'No.'

She smiled. 'If anyone had said to me you were domesticated, I would've laughed. But look at this place. It's spotless. And you even laundered all the new linen.'

'Ah.' He waved his fork at her in protest. 'I cook, because I enjoy it. I'm tidy, because if you live out of a suitcase, a mess means you leave things behind. But I don't do ironing. I use a laundry service.'

'Are you telling me you got a laundry to do the sheets and towels?'

He shrugged. 'Makes sense.'

'Maybe when you didn't have your own place. But you do now. And we have a washing machine and a tumble-dryer.'

We.

Jane suddenly realised that Mitch was making a huge compromise—he'd spent years living out of a suitcase, but now he'd made a settled base. For her.

So maybe this meant he was starting to accept the baby. Even though he still refused to talk about it and changed the subject when anyone mentioned nurseries or her bump.

Maybe everything would be all right.

He rolled his eyes. 'I loathe ironing. It's a complete waste of time. So although I'm fine with cooking and doing my share of the chores, I don't iron.'

'Real men don't iron, hmm?' She burst out laughing.

'This one doesn't.'

Something in his eyes warned her to stop teasing him. So she changed the subject, kept things light. He didn't let her wash up, either.

'I'm not an invalid. I'm expecting a baby.'

'I know. But you've already done a lot today. Go and sit down.'

'Territorial about the kitchen, are you?'

'No.' He flapped a tea towel at her. 'Just go and sit down. Otherwise I'll ring Charlie and tell her you're overdoing things.'

'That's blackmail.'

'Yeah. And it'd get me Brownie points,' he said with a grin. 'Shoo.'

He curled up on the sofa with her for the rest of the evening—just chilling out, listening to music and holding her close.

If they spent time together like this, Jane thought, then soon he'd start to open up. Talk to her about the baby. Share. She was sure of it.

And then it was time for bed. After a shower, she climbed

in, feeling odd. She was used to her narrow single bed. The king-sized mattress felt huge.

'OK?' he asked, climbing in next to her.

'Yes. I'm just not used to so much space. And it's… well, it's a strange bed.'

He shrugged. 'I'm used to it. Different motel each night, when I'm in Tornado Alley. Some are better than others.' He settled back against the pillows and picked up what looked like a scientific manuscript and a red pen.

'You're working?'

'Huh?' He looked at her. 'Oh. Sorry. Is the light disturbing you?'

'No. I just…' Hadn't expected him to start working. The nights she'd spent with him before, he'd cuddled her to sleep.

Were things going to be different now that they'd actually moved in together?

When she'd turned her pillow over and shifted position for the tenth time, Mitch put down his paper. 'OK. I get the message.'

'I wasn't doing it on purpose,' she protested. 'I just…' She rubbed the small of her back, trying to do it surreptitiously so he wouldn't see.

But he saw anyway. 'You can't get comfortable. OK. Face the other way and I'll rub your back,' he said.

'That *wasn't* a hint,' she protested.

'Your back's clearly aching. And it's easier for me to do it than for you to struggle and try to do it yourself. Turn round.'

The touch of his hands was bliss. He knew just the right spot to rub, with the right pressure.

But she remembered the last time he'd given her a massage. It had led to lovemaking. And right now she was just too damned tired and aching. Despite what she'd promised the girls, she'd overdone it a bit today. She had an archivist's need to put everything in its right place.

'Relax, will you?' He kissed her shoulder.

'Last time you gave me a massage…'

'That was last time,' he said. 'Tonight, you're tired.' He nuzzled the sensitive spot at the curve of her neck. 'I know I said it'd be nice to christen the flat tonight, but there's always tomorrow morning. Sunday. When we don't have to rush.' Another kiss. 'And when it's going to be a whole lot better.'

He lived up to his promise. Jane spent the whole of Sunday with a smile on her face. And she was relaxing on the sofa that evening with a book and the stereo on when he came into the living room to collect a file.

'Are you working?' she asked. 'I'll turn the music down.'

'It's OK. I'll do this on the plane.'

'Plane?' She put her book down and followed him into the bedroom.

He was packing.

'Where are you going?' she asked.

'Back to my job. I told you I was only here for a week.'

But…he'd got the flat for them. Hadn't that meant he was going to stay a bit longer?

The question must have been written over her face, because he said, 'I won't be away that long. I'll try and get back as soon as I can.'

'When's your flight?'

'Eleven tomorrow.'

When she'd be at work. And they were short-staffed, so it wouldn't be fair to ring Stella and ask for extra leave. Throwing a sickie was absolutely out of the question. So she wasn't even going to get to wave him off. 'Right.'

'Jane, don't make an issue out of this,' he warned. 'You knew it was going to be like this.'

Maybe she had. But by Wednesday she was starting to feel lonely. Even though Mitch called her every day. Even though he sent her emails and pictures. It wasn't the same as actually sharing her space with him. And if her parents hadn't put her in boarding-school and her mother had stayed at home while her father went from dig to dig, this was exactly what life would've been like when she was growing up. Seeing her mother put a brave face on it but missing her husband all the while.

And even Jane's job didn't distract her. She was planning an exhibition, choosing the documents they were going to highlight; in the evenings, she worked on the copy to give to the design agency for the backdrops, but the second she switched off her laptop she was aware of the space around her. The silence. The *loneliness*.

'What's up?' Hannah asked when she came with Jane to the next antenatal appointment.

'Nothing.' Jane gave her a brilliant smile.

'I've known you long enough to tell,' Hannah said. 'And if you're upset about something, it won't be good for the baby. So what's really wrong?'

Jane sighed. 'I feel like a selfish cow.'

Hannah scoffed. 'Since when?'

'Mitch sorted the flat out for us.'

'And you're not happy there? Horrible neighbours?' Hannah guessed.

'No, they're fine.' Jane sighed again. 'But I'm used to you lot being around. Mitch has been away for two weeks and I've no idea when he's coming back or how long he'll stay, next time round.' She bit her lip. 'This is stupid. But I'm lonely,' she admitted.

'Oh, honey.' Hannah gave her a hug. 'Look, you know we're always pleased to see you. And we'll keep coming round to yours, too.' She paused. 'But that's treating the symptom, not the cause of the problem.'

Jane nodded. 'It's always going to be like this. He'll be back for a week and it'll be brilliant, and then he'll be gone for however long. I don't want this for me. And I definitely don't want this for my baby.'

'You need to talk to him about it,' Hannah advised gently.

'When he gets back,' Jane agreed. 'I need to do this in person.'

But another week dragged by, and even though the girls insisted on her going over to their place for dinner, or brought a film and a huge bag of popcorn over to her flat, when it was back to being just her and the bump, the place just seemed to echo.

And she hated it.

The following week, Jane was working on the exhibition materials when she heard the sound of a key in the lock. Then the door closed, and she heard a deep voice call, 'Anyone home?'

'In here.'

There was a thud—which she assumed was his suitcase in the hall—and then he came into the living room.

Her heart missed a beat. She'd forgotten just how gorgeous he was. Especially when he smiled like that. A warm, sexy smile that promised pure pleasure.

She stood up, and he slid his arms round her. Kissed her. Though what started out soft and gentle turned rapidly into hot and needy, and he carried her straight to bed. All thoughts of discussing the situation went straight out of her head as he touched her, kissed her, stroked her from arousal to white heat.

'Mmm. That was a nice welcome home,' he said afterwards, when her head was resting on his shoulder and her arm was slung round his waist.

'You didn't even say hello.'

'Yes, I did. Just not in words.' His voice was filled with laughter. 'And not in the same way I'd greet anyone else.'

'Glad to hear it.' Though it hadn't occurred to her before. Mitch travelled around a lot. He must meet women all the time. Women who didn't have an enormous bump. Women who'd see just how attractive he was and want to get to know him better.

And despite the fact that her bump had really grown since he'd last seen her, he hadn't said a word about that, either.

'Don't tense up on me. What's the matter?' he asked.

'Nothing. You didn't say you were coming back.'

'I wanted to surprise you. Except the flowers at the airport were—well—I'll buy you some tomorrow.'

She didn't want flowers. She wanted *him.*

'Which reminds me. I brought you something. Hang on.' He climbed out of bed, pulled on his boxer shorts and padded barefoot from the room.

Things had definitely changed around here, Mitch thought. He'd left a flat that was comfortable and functional. But while he'd been away Jane had bought plants. Hung prints on the walls. There were postcards on a pinboard in the kitchen and what looked like several pots of herbs on the window sill. Cushions on the sofa. A vase of flowers on the window sill. Candles on the mantelpiece.

For a moment, panic clenched his gut. It felt like *home*. And he wasn't used to this—he lived out of short-let flats here and motels when he was in the States. He was never in one place too long, whereas this was a six-month let with an option to renew.

It felt like putting down roots.

Just as he'd done before.

Natalie's style had been very different—Jane, despite her teasing about hot pink, had kept things to neutral colours and sunny yellows, and there were prints of old maps on the walls instead of the modern art he'd shared with Natalie. But the flat held the same warm feeling as the little terraced house in Cambridge he'd bought with Natalie—the house he couldn't quite bring himself to sell, but he'd not been able to live there either, so he'd rented it out.

He was going to have to tell Jane about what had happened, he knew. But the longer he left it, the harder it got. And the baby was showing now. Really showing. How could he tell Jane something that would worry her and give her nightmares?

On the other hand, how could he not?

Ah, hell. One day at a time. Keep things in the here and now, on an even keel, he reminded himself, and fished for the little box in his suitcase.

The box he held out with a smile was much too big to hold a ring. And it was stupid of her to even entertain the idea, Jane told herself crossly. He didn't know her ring size, and he wasn't going to ask her to marry him. That would mean commitment, and she'd begun to realise just how scared Mitch was of commitment. The fact he'd rented this flat for them was more than she could have expected. To hope for any more would be foolish in the extreme.

'Thank you,' she said, accepting the box and opening it. Inside was a strange shape. 'Sorry to show my ignorance. What is it?'

'A fulgurite.'

'I'm still none the wiser.'

'Fossilised lightning.'

'I thought lightning was an electrical force. And it comes from the atmosphere. So how can it be fossilised?'

He sat on the edge of the bed. 'A lightning bolt contains around a gigajoule of energy—that's enough to power a home for a week. When a force like that hits the sand, the heat's incredible; it melts the minerals in the sand and fuses them. And that's what a fulgurite is—a hollow tube of melted sand, made by a lightning strike. I thought you'd like it.'

'I do. Thank you.' She looked at it again, intrigued. 'Did you find this yourself?'

'No. But I did discover a little shop that sells them. By the way, it's very, very fragile, so it's probably best kept in its box.'

'It's beautiful. How do people find them?'

'Excavation. Similar to the methods archaeologists use.'

He knew what her parents did. Was this his way of asking if she'd told her parents? Was he prepared to talk to his, now?

She decided to test the waters. Carefully. 'Dad would be fascinated by this.'

And this was where he said that of course, now he remembered: her parents were archaeologists. How were they and how had they taken the news that they'd be grandparents?

But nothing. He seemed perfectly happy to keep the conversation on non-emotional matters. About fulgurites—where they were found, and what effect the soil structure had on them. It was all interesting stuff, and normally she would've enjoyed talking about it. But right now it was yet another barrier between them. An excuse not to focus on the fact that she was getting on for nearly halfway through her pregnancy and nothing was really settled.

If she let it, this week could be just like the last one. Going out, doing things together, falling asleep in his arms, making love with him until her whole body felt fluid. Then he'd leave, and she'd realise that yet again they hadn't discussed the situation.

So maybe she'd better do this up front. 'How long are you back for?'

He climbed back into bed. 'A week or so.'

She sighed. 'And then you're leaving me on my own *again*.'

'You're not on your own. You've got the girls just round the corner,' he pointed out.

'It's not the same.' She kept her gaze fixed on his. 'Do you know, this is the first time I've ever lived on my own?'

He blinked. 'And the problem is?'

'I'm used to people being around me. I went to boarding-school, I lived in halls of residence at university, and when I started work I house-shared with the girls. So I'm not used to being on my own all the time—where there's nobody to have a coffee with or chat to, nobody else making a noise in the house.'

'I still don't see the problem.'

'Because you're used to moving around. Being on your own. I'm not.' She felt her mouth thin into a line. 'And I'm not being a wimp, before you say it. I know I'm perfectly capable of coping on my own. But I'm used to being around people and I'm lonely, Mitch. I'm seventeen weeks pregnant, and I don't want to be on my own. Just in case something happens.'

His face shuttered. 'Nothing's going to happen. Everything's going to be fine.'

She really didn't understand why he was so stubborn about this. Why he refused to discuss it. Unless something had happened in his past—but if that was the case, why hadn't he told her?

She really, really didn't understand what went on in Mitch Holland's head.

'I need a coffee. I'll get you a drink,' he said, and left the room. Jane didn't have the energy to follow him. When he brought the drink back to her, he was all smiles again—and he switched the subject away from his absences and the baby. And somehow she couldn't get the conversation to turn back to what was really important.

During the week, she noticed that he didn't even pick up one of the pregnancy magazines she'd stacked on the coffee-table. And although he was as affectionate and warm towards her as she could have asked him to be—and she was particularly glad he didn't stop touching her because of the bump—she was aware that he was evading the subject of the baby. Here and now was fine; laughter and lovemaking were fine. But he wouldn't make plans for the future and it drove her crazy. She didn't want to leave everything until the last minute.

'This is the time we ought to be planning,' she said, later that evening.

'What?'

'While I'm in the second trimester. When it's easier to do things and I feel great. When I'm not spending half my time with my head down the toilet, and while I'm not waddling everywhere or too tired to do anything.'

'Planning what?'

Was he being deliberately dense? 'For the baby. Nursery furniture.'

He waved a dismissive hand. 'There's plenty of time.'

'Mitch, we need to get things ordered. A pram. Car seats. All that sort of stuff.'

'There's plenty of time. And it's tempting fate to plan too early.'

Something about his tone alerted her. 'You're the one who said I was being silly, worrying about being on my own when I'm pregnant. So are you saying you think something might happen?'

'No, just that it's not the right time.' Though she noticed he didn't meet her eyes.

'So when is the right time?'

'Jane. I'm jet-lagged.'

No way. He'd been back for four days.

'Can we have this conversation when I've caught up on my sleep?'

It made her feel guilty, as if she were in the wrong, when she knew she wasn't. But she'd try again, because they really had to sort this out.

On Friday, she cooked them a special meal. And when he seemed relaxed and in a good mood, she brought up the subject again. 'Mitch. We really need to talk. This flat...'

'What's wrong with the flat?'

'Nothing. But...look, when the baby comes, we're going to need things for him.'

'Him?' He blinked. 'The baby's a boy?'

'I don't know, but I'm not calling our baby "it".'

He was silent. Then he shrugged. 'If you're not happy with the flat, find something you *do* like. We'll move.'

'To another rented flat?'

'What's wrong with that?'

'Mitch, I'm having a baby. Our baby,' she clarified. 'I want to be settled.'

'We are settled. The lease here is renewable. And unless you suddenly become the neighbour from hell by playing music full blast at three in the morning, slamming doors and throwing rubbish into the neighbours' gardens, there won't be a problem renewing it.'

'Renting feels *temporary*.'

'You want to buy somewhere?'

At the shock on his face, she backtracked slightly. 'I just want to feel settled.'

'You *are* settled.'

You, she noticed. Not *we*. 'But you're never here.'

'My job means travelling. You know that.'

'And when you are here you won't discuss things.'

'What things?'

'There's so much we've left unsorted. Have you told your parents about the baby, yet?'

He shook his head.

'Why not? Aren't you close to them?'

'Close enough.'

More prevarication. It was enough to make her snap. 'You never talk about your family. I know nothing about them other than that your mum teaches domestic science and you have a sister who loves shopping. I've never even seen their photographs, for pity's sake!'

'Look, it's fine. I'll talk to them soon.'

Not specific enough. 'When do I get to meet them?'

'Soon.'

She refused to let him fob her off. 'Why don't you invite them here for Sunday lunch?'

'This Sunday?'

She could hear the faint note of panic in his voice, and although it made her feel horrible she knew she had to push this. For her baby's sake. 'Yes.'

'I can't. I'm flying back to the States.'

'What? I thought you were here for a couple of weeks?' He hadn't been specific about how long he was staying—but surely he'd planned to tell her more than two days before he left?'

'I had a call from Brad today.'

'Who's Brad?'

'My number two on the project. There's a problem. He needs me to sort it out.'

'Why can't he do it?'

'Because I have more experience.'

'And you're the only person in the world who could fix the problem?' She shook her head in disbelief. 'Why does this feel as if you're running away?'

'Because you're paranoid.'

She sighed. 'Mitch, you won't discuss *anything* about the future.'

'What's to discuss? Everything's fine.'

No, it wasn't. 'You won't even talk about baby names.'

'Because it's unlucky to discuss it in advance. Stop *worrying*.' He pushed his chair back, scooped her from hers, sat down in her place and settled her on his lap. 'Everything's going to be fine.'

She let him distract her with kisses—kisses that quickly led to her losing most of her clothes and him carrying her to bed. But only because he'd put up such a huge wall between them, she had no idea how else to scale it. At least in bed he let her close. And maybe, just maybe, if she kept close to him, he'd learn to trust her enough to start demolishing that wall.

CHAPTER TEN

MITCH glanced at the display on his phone before he answered it. An international number?

His heart missed a beat. Jane never called him. They had a tacit agreement that he'd call her, when he was having a break and it was still a reasonable time in the UK.

So if Jane was ringing him…that meant something was wrong.

He stifled the panic. Of course not. He was just being paranoid. It was probably Harry chasing him up for something he'd forgotten. Everything was fine. He answered the call. 'Mitch Holland.'

'Mitch, it's Hannah. Jane's friend.'

The one who was a nurse. He went cold. 'What's happened?'

'Jane's in hospital. Don't panic, everything's going to be OK—but she had a bit of a scare.'

He could barely force the words out. 'What sort of scare? Is she all right? Is the baby all right?'

'She had a bit of a bleed.'

Bleed.

Pictures of Natalie flashed into his head. 'Oh, my God.'

'It's OK, Mitch. I took her in myself. She's going to be fine, and I was there when they did a scan to check the baby. They're just keeping her in for observation for a couple of days. To be on the safe side.'

He dragged in a breath. He still couldn't get past the word 'bleed'. And even though the rational part of his brain knew it wasn't the same thing that happened to Natalie, he couldn't stop the panic. Hot, choking panic that made him feel as if he couldn't breathe, as if he were going to be violently sick. 'Is…?'

'Everything's OK,' Hannah reassured him. 'She just wanted you to know. And obviously she can't ring you from hospital.'

This was where he was meant to send a message back. But he couldn't think what to say, beyond a lame, 'Thank you.' His brain had completely deserted him.

He was still shaking when he ended the call.

Part of him wanted to stay here, where he'd be so busy focusing on work that he wouldn't have time to think about the situation. But the better part of him knew that he'd never be able to forgive himself if he let Jane down. And this time there wasn't a white-out to stop him. There was no reason why he couldn't get on a plane and fly back to London. Walk into that hospital. Be there for Jane when she needed his support.

His mother's voice echoed in his head. *When are you going to forgive yourself, Mitch?*

He wasn't sure he ever could. But he also knew he couldn't bear the same sort of thing on his conscience all over again. Regardless of the fact that they were in the middle of something important right now, he'd put Jane before his job.

He flipped open his phone, retrieved Hannah's number from the call list and rang her straight back. 'Hannah? It's Mitch. I'm on my way back. Which hospital?'

'London City General. Maternity ward. Her consultant's Kieran Bailey.'

'Thanks. Tell Jane I'll be there as soon as I can get a flight.'

'OK.'

He snapped the phone closed, and went to find Brad.

'I was just coming to get you,' Brad said with a grin. 'We have a beauty forming over here. Look at this!' He showed Mitch the screen.

Usually, the adrenalin rush would start now. He'd be as excited as the rest of the team, dying to get out there and watch the tornado form. Track it. Collect the data and see how it fitted his theories.

But not today.

'Sorry, mate, you're on your own.'

'What?' Brad frowned. 'What do you mean, on my own?'

'I mean that you're in charge. I have to go back to London.'

Something in his tone must have alerted his colleague, because instead of making a fuss Brad asked, 'Everything OK?'

'Don't know until I get there.' Mitch sucked in a breath. 'I'm sorry to let you down like this—but I really do have to go.'

'Any idea when you'll be back?'

'As soon as.' Mitch sighed, knowing he owed his colleague a proper explanation—and appreciating the fact that Brad had given him space instead of pushing. 'Jane's in hospital. Her friend's a nurse—she says it's going to be all right, but I need to see her for myself.'

'Oh, no. I'm sorry.'

'It's not just her.' Mitch forced himself to say the rest. The first time he'd acknowledged it to anyone else apart from Jane and Harry. 'It's the baby. I'll be in touch when I can, OK?'

'Baby?'

Mitch closed his eyes. 'Baby. We're having a baby in January.'

'January? No wonder you've been hopping back and forth over the pond. And first babies—this is your first baby?'

Yes and no. But it was easier to nod.

'They're always… Well. I know what I was like with my own. Fussing so much that I drove Deanna crazy.' Brad smiled at him and clapped his shoulder. 'Try not to worry too much. I'm sure everything will be OK. We'll be rooting for you.'

'Do you mind not telling the others? Just in case…' Mitch couldn't say the rest. He didn't want to tempt fate.

Just please, please, let everything be all right.

Given the choice of waiting six hours for a direct flight, or taking a longer journey with several changes that would get him to London two hours earlier, Mitch picked the long haul. Though he was too keyed up to sleep, and he drank way too much coffee. He managed to get through to Harry in the wait between one of the airline changes, and she promised to book him a taxi straight from the airport to the hospital.

Which meant he stumbled through the door of London City General at four a.m. Kansas time—when everyone in the UK was bright and cheerful at ten in the morning. He just about had enough English money on him to buy Jane some flowers from the hospital shop. And then he walked into the maternity unit—needing a shave, with bloodshot eyes and his clothes creased from travelling.

No wonder the midwives were frowning at him.

One of them walked over to him. 'Can I help you?' she asked, sounding polite yet wary.

'I'm here to see Jane Redmond.'

'Are you family?'

Was she going to refuse to let him see Jane? His eyes narrowed. 'I've spent the past sixteen hours travelling from America. I know I look a mess and I could do with a shower and a shave—but no way am I moving from here until I've seen her for myself and know she's OK. And the baby.'

'I still need to ask the question.'

Her voice was cool and calm, but it sounded as if she had him pegged as trouble, a nutter, or both. He had to defuse the situation, and fast. He put both hands up in a gesture of surrender. 'I'm sorry. I don't mean to be rude. It's just that I've had one hell of a journey and I'm worried sick about Jane.

I'm…' What? Her live-in lover? 'The father of her baby.' It was the first time he'd said it out loud. 'I know her consultant's name is Kieran Bailey, if that helps.' He glanced at her badge. Senior Midwife. 'I'm Mitch. Mitch Holland. And I…'

He had to swallow hard. Because he was that close to falling to his knees and sobbing his heart out. 'Please. I really need to see her for myself.'

'I'll check with her.' She motioned to him to wait in a corridor, and walked into a little side room. A few moments later, she came back. 'Jane says she'll see you. Go in. But she needs to rest, OK?'

He nodded. 'Thank you. I could hug you for that.'

'No need.' She waved him into the room.

And Jane looked so pale, so small. He put the flowers on her bedside cabinet. 'Are you all right?'

She stared at him. 'Why are you here? Don't you have a storm to chase?'

He strove for lightness. 'You could say I'm taking a rain check. Or even a tornado check.'

'Not funny.'

'I know.' He sat on the edge of the bed and took her hand. Pressed a kiss into the palm.

'You look like hell,' she said.

'I feel it,' he admitted. 'I've been travelling for sixteen hours and I couldn't sleep.' Couldn't rest until he'd seen her. Again, he tried to keep it light. 'And I'm not sure what day it is or what time it is.' Though that was true rather than a joke. 'What happened?'

'I started spotting. I thought I was going to l—' Her breath hitched, but he knew exactly what she was going to say. She'd thought she was going to lose the baby.

Not caring whether it was against the rules or not, he moved nearer and wrapped his arms round her. Held her tightly, hoping she could draw strength from him. Let her cry over him.

And eventually her shudders stopped for long enough for

Mitch to let her go again. He poured her a glass of water and handed it to her. 'Just take small sips,' he said gently, and took the glass away again when she'd had enough. 'Hannah said everything was all right. But I needed to see you for myself.'

Her expression said she didn't believe him.

'Are you really all right?'

She nodded.

'So what made you start spotting?'

'It's what they call an abruption. A small tear in the placenta. It just happens sometimes—it's nothing I did wrong, and I haven't been lifting anything heavy at work either, before you ask.'

'I know,' he soothed. 'You're sensible. So what now? Do you need an operation or anything?'

'No, they said it wasn't too bad a tear and it should heal itself. The baby's fine, too.' She grimaced. 'Except I need bedrest for the next week. So I'm moving in with the girls again.'

'Why?'

She rolled her eyes. 'Isn't it obvious? Because I don't want to be on my own. Just in case…'

Although she didn't finish the sentence, he knew what she was telling him. 'It could happen again?'

'Hopefully not.' She bit her lip. 'Anyway. They're letting me out tomorrow and Hannah's going to take the morning off so she can pick up some stuff for me from the flat.'

The flat, he noticed. Not *our flat*. Or *home*.

'But Hannah has to work,' he pointed out. 'Shelley's a teacher so she can't just take time off during term time. And Charlie has to work, too. So you're not going to have anyone with you, most of the time.'

'Better than being on my own *all* the time,' she pointed out.

He rubbed the pad of his thumb over the back of her hand. 'I don't want you back in that tiny bed. No way are you going to be comfortable. Especially now.'

'It's better than being on my own,' she repeated.

'You're not going to be on your own. I'll take time off.'

This time, she really did scoff. *'You?'*

'Yes, me. And I can make sure you stay in bed.'

She shook her head. 'Mitch, I really don't think sex is a good idea right now.'

He rolled his eyes. 'That's not what I meant at all. I'm perfectly capable of sharing a bed with you without having sex with you. Which isn't the same as saying I think you're no longer desirable because of the bump, before you start thinking that. But it's my place to look after you.'

She stared at him. 'You're doing this out of duty?'

'No. Don't twist my words.' He raked a hand through his hair. 'I'm jet-lagged and sleep-deprived and I don't have a clue what I'm saying. Except that I'm going to look after you. And I mean that. I want to do it.'

'You're actually going to take time off work?'

He nodded. 'Until you're better.'

'But aren't you…?'

'In the middle of something? Yes.' He shrugged. 'It'll have to wait.'

She swallowed. 'And when I'm better?'

'Let's just concentrate on getting you well,' he said. 'I'm going home to crash for a couple of hours. I'll come back and see you later this afternoon. Anything you need me to bring?'

She shook her head. 'I'm fine.'

'OK. Ring me if you change your mind. Don't worry about waking me up—if you need me, I'm here.' He kissed her lightly. 'And I'm glad everything's OK.'

Mitch was as good as his word. He reappeared later that afternoon, still looking as if he needed sleep, but he'd shaved, showered and changed. And he brought Jane some grapes and a couple of magazines. 'Just to keep you going this evening. What time can I come and pick you up tomorrow?'

'The consultant's seeing me at ten.'

'Do you need me to be here?'

Yes. But she wasn't going to push it. 'No, that's fine. I should be ready by about half past.'

'I'll be here.' He stayed with her until the end of visiting time, then reappeared the following morning at exactly half past ten. He insisted that she waited in the foyer while he fetched the car. And she blinked in surprise when she saw what he was driving: not a flashy sports car, this time, but a sensible family car.

'You hired *this*?'

'It's easier for you to get in and out of than a low-slung car with bucket seats,' he said with a shrug.

He'd actually thought of her, put her needs before his own wants. Hired a car he probably loathed instead of the fast, sleek machines he loved.

She was near to tears as she climbed in. And her eyes filled again when she walked into the flat and discovered that, not only had he tidied everything, he'd changed the bed linen and put the washing machine on, he'd stocked the fridge, he'd bought some extra pillows, and he'd moved the TV into the bedroom.

'Bedrest means staying put. And although this lot will keep you busy for a while—' he indicated the pile of books and puzzle magazines on her bedside table '—you're going to get seriously bored if you're stuck in one place for a week. So just in case you wanted to watch a film or something…'

There was a pile of DVDs next to the books. All very girly films, she noticed: costume dramas and romantic comedies. The sort of thing he'd never want to watch in a million years.

He'd be bored, bored, bored.

Or else he'd work in the living room. Jane couldn't imagine him actually keeping her company, especially since he was having to take time off work. Oh, well. At least she'd be able to call out to him if there was a problem.

'Get into bed,' he said, pulling the duvet to one side.

By the time she'd stripped off and got into bed, he'd made her a drink. And then he actually came to sit with her; she really hadn't expected that. But he chatted with her. Made her lunch and brought it through on a tray. He didn't discuss the baby at all, but at least he was talking to her. Spending time with her.

And to Jane's surprise he didn't get bored or go off to work in the living room over the next week. He kept her company. He played board games with her, cheated outrageously at Scrabble and had her laughing so much she forgot to worry about the abruption and whether the baby was OK, watched films with her, or just held her while she slept.

He didn't complain once, even though she asked him if being here was putting the project behind or causing problems with his work; he merely said he had it covered and she wasn't to worry about anything. The only time he left the flat was to do some shopping—and even then it was only when one of the girls was there, to make sure she didn't get out of bed or start doing something.

'I'm sure that it'd be OK for me to get up and get dressed. I can't loll around in bed in a nightie all week,' she said.

'Bedrest means what it says.' He gave her a sidelong glance that heated her blood. 'And I like having you in nothing but a nightie. As soon as you're better we'll have a lot of making up to do…'

Oh-h-h. The pictures that raised in her mind.

'Stop it,' he said giving her a sultry grin. 'Or I'm going to need a cold shower.'

'Stop what?'

'Looking at me like that. I'm going to make myself a cup of coffee and you a herbal tea. And when I walk back in here, I want you demure.'

She laughed. 'And if I'm not?'

'Then I'll have a cold shower, then make you watch science fiction films for the rest of the day,' he threatened, laughing.

She liked this side of him. This light-hearted, sexy, teasing man.

Towards the end of the week, they were lying in bed, talking, and Jane held him close. 'Thank you for looking after me like this. You've been brilliant. I didn't expect you to come back when Hannah rang you.'

'You think I'm that awful?'

His voice was even, not outraged, and she realised she'd hurt him. She stroked his cheek. 'No. Just that you haven't really accepted the…situation.' Oh, God. He had her at it now, avoiding the B-word.

'It's been hard for me,' he admitted.

'Want to talk about it?'

'About what?'

'Whatever's on your mind.' She ran her hand down his side. 'You're all tense.'

'It's my new job—my new boss. I have to wait on this woman hand and foot and she's terribly demanding—runs me ragged,' he said lightly.

But she knew he was trying to tease her, change the subject. This time, she had a feeling it was important. That it was time to push. She stroked his hair back from his forehead. 'Tell me,' she said softly.

He sighed. 'I don't know whether to or not. I don't want to upset you.'

She went very still. 'You're involved with someone else?'

'No, of *course* not.' He sighed again. 'Just don't take this the wrong way.'

She was really worried now. She needed to know. 'Tell me.'

'Two years ago, I was engaged. To Natalie. I'd known her since I was a student. We worked together for a while—she was a meteorologist, too. Then I had the chance to go to Antarctica for six months to expand on the research I'd done for my PhD.'

She stared at him. 'You've got a doctorate?' And he'd never

told her. He didn't use his title, either, because any letters delivered for him had been addressed to Mr Holland, not Dr Holland.

'It's irrelevant.'

Yes, and she didn't want to distract him. 'OK. Go on.'

'I talked it over with Natalie, and she said I should go—it was the perfect opportunity and it'd be good for my career. It was only for six months and although we'd miss each other, we'd cope.'

His eyes had gone dark, haunted, and there were lines etched into his face. Painful memories, Jane guessed.

'I'd been at the base for a month when Natalie called me. She told me we were going to have a baby. I guess we got a bit carried away on my last night in England. We hadn't planned it to happen.'

'And you hated the idea of being tied down?' Was this what it was all about? He already had a child he never saw?

He shook his head. 'It wasn't that at all. We were getting married anyway—the church was booked for the month after I came back from Antarctica. So it didn't matter—maybe I could get leave and we could bring the wedding forward, or we could put it back until after the baby arrived. I thought we had plenty of time to decide what we wanted to do. And the more I thought about it, the more I liked the idea of being a dad. I was twenty-eight. Just about ready to settle down and start a family.'

He wore no wedding ring and he lived out of a suitcase, not with his wife and toddler—so clearly something had gone badly wrong. Had Natalie found someone else while he was in Antarctica? Had she been unable to put up with all the travelling and divorced him?

A muscle flickered in his jaw. 'Three weeks later…' His voice was raw with pain. 'Three weeks later, my mum called me. Natalie was dead.'

It was the last thing Jane had expected. 'What? Oh, Mitch. I…' Her voice tailed off and she shook her head. 'I don't know what to say.' Sorry wasn't enough. It wasn't anywhere near enough. All she could do was hold him. Let him know that she was there for him.

'I haven't finished yet.'

There was more?

His breath hitched. 'It seemed she had an ectopic pregnancy. It ruptured her Fallopian tube. And she died on the operating table.'

'Oh, my God.' No wonder he'd acted the way he did. Her news must have brought it all back to him. The way he'd felt on discovering that the woman he loved was expecting his child. The joy of learning that they'd made a new life together. And then the nightmare when it had all gone so badly wrong.

And no wonder he'd come straight back from America when Hannah had told him she was in hospital after a bleed. A placental abruption wasn't the same thing as an ectopic pregnancy, but it carried similar dangers. And both involved bleeding.

'Mitch, I…' Her voice faded. What could she say to him? He'd lost everything. Nothing would make that all right. Nothing at all.

'Oh, it gets worse,' he said, his voice bitter. 'There was a blizzard—a bad one. I couldn't leave the base until it had stopped. It was too dangerous for a pilot to bring a plane in, and there wasn't a chance in hell of getting off the base any other way. I was willing to walk it, but my boss pointed out that he wasn't prepared to send any of the team with me or the dogs, and if I went alone they'd end up having to send a search party to find me—I'd be risking other people's lives.' He dragged in a breath. 'I had enough blood on my hands already. So what could I do but stay put? We were stuck there for *days*. And I didn't even manage to make it home for the funeral. I couldn't pay her the tribute she deserved.' His eyes glittered. 'I can't forgive myself for that.'

'It wasn't your fault that you couldn't get back. You were snowed in. And it wasn't your fault that Natalie died.'

'If I'd been in England, instead of in Antarctica, I would've been with Natalie when she felt the first pain. I would've driven her to hospital. And it would've been early enough to save her.'

'I didn't know her, so I can't say anything meaningful,' Jane said. 'But I'm sorry you had to go through something so painful. And I'm sorry that I've reopened the wounds.' It explained why he chased storms, too. The risks wouldn't mean anything to him. Not after what had happened. He didn't care about anything, any more. Didn't want to let himself care, in case he lost everything all over again.

'It's not your fault. But when you told me you were pregnant, it brought everything back. I just…shut off.'

To stop himself hurting. To keep the memories and the pain from drowning him.

Now she knew about his past, she could understand why he'd reacted that way. At the time she'd thought it was because he was too selfish to care; now she knew it was because he cared too much. And because he was terrified the nightmare might happen again.

'So now you know the truth. I'm sorry. I know I haven't behaved the way I should've done. I've been running away instead of supporting you. Sticking my head in the sand and pretending it isn't happening.'

'Refusing to discuss the baby or make plans.'

'I made plans last time. I was going to try to cut my project short so I could be there for all the antenatal appointments. I spent all my free time on Internet sites about pregnancy and baby names. I planned how I was going to paint the nursery. This time, I didn't want to do anything. In case I jinxed…' He dragged in a breath, clearly not wanting to say it aloud. 'And when Hannah called me…'

He'd been reminded of what had happened to Natalie. Worried that it was going to happen all over again. And since his first reaction had been to drop everything and come to her side…then maybe there was hope. Despite the barriers he'd tried to put up, he cared. So maybe he wasn't going to keep going away and putting distance between them.

'It's all right,' she said softly. 'Everything's going to be just fine. We'll get through this. Together.'

CHAPTER ELEVEN

THE following day, Mitch finally allowed Jane to get up—just for the morning—but he still didn't let her do anything in the flat.

'This is ridiculous,' she said. 'I hardly even know what day it is.' Then she looked at the calendar. 'Ah.'

'What?'

'I'm due at the hospital tomorrow.'

'A follow-up from last week?'

'No.' She took his hand and squeezed it. Smiled at him. 'I'm going to ask you something now. Will you come with me?'

'To the appointment?'

'It's the scan,' she said. 'And the kind of scan they do at London City General is the three-D one.'

'Three-D?'

'The one I sent you a photograph of—from the dating scan—was a two-D scan. Just a side-on view. But this one's a lot more detailed. It means,' she said softly, 'you actually get to see our baby's face.'

Panic skittered over his expression.

'Look, I know you don't want to make plans. And I know why, so I'm not going to push you any more about painting a nursery and picking names and what have you. But it would mean a lot to me if you came with me to the scan.'

'Part of me wants to. But part of me doesn't. I'm not rejecting you or the baby, I swear I'm not.' He dragged in a breath. 'This just scares the hell out of me. If I let myself love this baby, if I let myself think about the future...what if it all goes wrong again?'

'Nobody can guarantee everything's going to work out. But you have to believe, Mitch. See the glass as half full. And think about it. The chances of something going wrong, weighed against the chances of everything being fine—the odds are in our favour.'

'I know. Intellectually, I know that. But there's a world of difference between what I know in my head and the way I feel,' he admitted.

'Then that's even more of a reason to come to the scan. So you can see for yourself that everything is fine.'

He sighed. 'I'll think about it, OK?'

It was frustrating, but she decided to stop pushing; if she insisted now, she knew it'd make him back away again. Hopefully if he thought about it he'd realise she was right. He'd come to the scan. And then—please, then—he'd finally be able to bond with their baby.

Mitch drove Jane to the hospital, the following day. Taking her to hospital wasn't obliging him to going into the scan with her—to taking that last step of commitment. She hadn't asked him again, so he knew she wouldn't push.

He also knew she'd be hugely disappointed if he waited for her outside. And he'd already disappointed her enough in this pregnancy. But he still couldn't get past the fear. The conviction that if he bonded with this baby, if he risked giving his heart again, everything would all go wrong again.

He parked the car and walked into the clinic with her. He waited while she was weighed and gave a urine sample; and although the waiting was interminable, the only magazines around were pregnancy magazines. Which he most definitely didn't want to read.

He glanced around the waiting room. How could the other fathers-to-be look so calm? Or were they, like him, outwardly quiet and serene and inwardly in turmoil? Panicking that they'd lose their partner or the baby?

And the fear rising in him wasn't just because of what had happened to Natalie. Jane's pregnancy hadn't exactly been problem-free. And although she was planning to go back to work later in the week, doing a half-day on Thursday and Friday to ease herself back in, he still worried. What if she had another abruption? A worse one?

It had been a mistake, looking up those medical sites. At three in the morning, unable to sleep and too tired to resist the lure, he'd looked up the condition and read the details. And his breathing had grown shallower and shallower as he'd realised what the complications could be. What the risks were.

He hadn't told Jane about it. And maybe he should've talked to Hannah, who might've been able to reassure him a bit, but no way could he have discussed it when Jane might overhear. She really didn't need that extra worry.

And then the radiographer called her name. 'Jane Redmond.'

This was it.

Crunch time.

Because once he'd walked through that door, there was no turning back. Even though he'd seen the picture Jane had sent him of the earlier scan, this time he'd see the baby on screen, moving as if a real person. And it wouldn't be just abstract any more. Wouldn't be the bump, something he could just not look at and pretend wasn't really there. It would be their baby.

Jane said nothing, just looked at him and waited to see if he'd stand up.

When he didn't, she said nothing, but her eyes were full of hurt. And her voice was cool when she said, 'I'll see you later, then.'

She was almost at the door when he caught her up. 'Jane.'

'What?'

He laced his fingers through hers. 'I'm sorry. I'm being an idiot.'

'Yes, you are.' Her voice was brisk but her eyes were suspiciously bright when he walked into the ultrasound room with her.

She lay back on the couch while the radiographer spread gel on her stomach. The scanner head picked up the signals and relayed them to the screen—and then he was looking at their child.

It was a two-dimensional black and white image, grainy but still recognisably a baby. He could see a head, arms, legs. Although the radiographer was talking and pointing things out, he wasn't really listening to what she was saying: all he could do was stare at the screen. At the baby.

'Mitch. *Mitch.*'

There was a hard jab in his side, and he glanced at Jane. 'Hmm?'

She nodded at their joined hands. 'You're hurting me.'

He hadn't even realised he was holding her hand that tightly, but his knuckles were white and he was clearly gripping her hand way too hard. He released her hand immediately. 'Sorry. I…' He dragged in a breath. 'Jane. That's our *baby*.'

'Uh-huh.'

He looked at the radiographer. 'Is everything all right? It's just this last week, with Jane being on bedrest and…'

'Everything's fine. I've checked the placenta and there's no sign of any further abruptions,' she reassured him, 'and the baby's growth is exactly on track. I was just saying to Mrs Redmond, there aren't any abnormalities in the heart or the brain or any of the other organs, there's no gap in the spine, and there are ten fingers and ten toes, so you can just relax and enjoy the rest of the pregnancy.' She smiled. 'You have a perfectly healthy baby, Mr Redmond.'

He didn't bother correcting her that his surname was Holland and that Jane wasn't Mrs anything; the names were irrelevant. The news, on the other hand, made him feel as if he were walking on air.

Everything was all right.

'Would you like to know the baby's sex?' the radiographer asked.

He looked at Jane. 'Do you?'

'If you do.'

He did, but he'd let her deal with most of her pregnancy alone, so far. He wasn't going to wade in and start throwing orders around. He needed to consider what *she* wanted. 'No, this is *your* choice.'

'Then, yes, I would like to know.'

'I'm delighted to tell you that you have a little girl,' the radiographer said with a smile.

'A little girl.' The words barely managed to get past the lump in his throat. 'Chloë,' he whispered.

'Now we've done the foetal anomaly scan, we can do the three-D option.' The radiographer flicked a switch, and suddenly the image changed. Became clearer. In colour.

Mitch was looking straight into the face of his little girl.

And she was smiling at him.

'She…she looks like you,' he said to Jane. 'But I think she's got my nose.'

His voice was full of wonder, and when Jane looked at Mitch she could see him blinking back the tears.

Pushing him into coming with her had been the right thing, after all.

Because now, finally, he was bonding with their baby—and everything was going to be all right.

The baby was sucking her thumb, now. Mitch looked at the radiographer. 'Is it possible to have a photograph, please?'

'And a DVD—that's what we call a four-D option. The fourth dimension is time, so you can see the baby moving. We put still pictures onto the DVD, as well.'

'This is amazing.' He shook his head. 'I take photographs for a living. Photographs of storms. They're powerful and energising and it's an incredible feeling, chasing a tornado and being part of something so elemental. But this…this is way beyond that.'

He stared at the screen, transfixed; throughout the rest of the scan, he was absolutely silent. Jane held his hand; his fingers tightened round hers, but this time not to a painful extent. And when the scan ended, he gently took a paper towel and wiped the gel from her stomach. Caressed the bump. And his eyes were very, very bright as he smiled at her.

The radiographer gave them their DVD and a folder of photographs, and they left; Mitch kept his arm round Jane all the way out of the hospital.

'That was just…' He shook his head, clearly lost for words. 'Our baby.'

She remembered the name he'd whispered to the screen. 'You want to call her Chloë?'

'It was just the first name that popped into my head.'

One he'd chosen before, with Natalie? Or had he, despite the fact he'd tried to block out what was happening, subconsciously been thinking about names?

'Chloë's fine by me. Though I think maybe we should include our mums' names as middle names,' she added.

'Fine. That's fine.' He stopped, and turned her to face him. 'Jane. Now I know everything's OK, I'm taking you somewhere.'

'Where?'

'Sussex.'

She looked at him. 'Why Sussex?'

'It's where my family lives.'

He was taking her to meet his family? She'd wanted that for so long—but she hadn't prepared for meeting them. Panic flared through her. 'We can't just turn up unannounced!'

'We're not going to. I'll call my mother and check they're going to be there before we go. Though as far as I know they're not away, and it's the school holidays so she should be there.' He smiled at her. 'We won't stay long. Lunch out, a walk on the beach, drop in to see them, and then back to London.'

She couldn't quite focus on what he was saying. 'Isn't it going to be a shock for your parents, meeting me and seeing…?' She indicated the bump.

'No, it'll be fine.' He smiled. 'Stop worrying. They'll be pleased.'

She sucked in a breath as another thought hit her. 'They won't see me as a substitute…?'

'For Natalie? No. And, for the record, my mother has been saying for a long, long time that it's time I forgave myself and moved on. They'll be really pleased to meet you.' He kissed her lightly. 'Stop worrying. Really. Or you'll end up back on bedrest.'

She groaned. 'If I have to spend another day stuck in bed…'

'I know. I'd go crazy, too. Though I only made you do it for your own good. And for our baby's sake.'

He was still saying it. *Our baby.* Pleasure rippled through her. He meant it. He really, really meant it.

He held her close. 'Can we show my parents the photos? The film?'

'Of course.' Part of her was stunned by the speed at which his attitude towards the baby had changed. But in a way she could understand it. He hadn't dared let himself get close in case it all went wrong; he'd kept the brakes on. But now he'd had reassurance from the radiographer that everything was fine, the brakes were off.

And Jane had seen the very second that Mitch had fallen in love with his daughter.

Hard.

She stifled the thought that he'd never said the L-word to her. He'd shown it, hadn't he? The fact he'd flown straight from America to come to her bedside when Hannah had called him had to mean something.

But all the same…it would've been nice to hear.

As soon as they were in the car, he made a quick phone call. And then he smiled at Jane. 'They're getting out the fatted calf.'

'Very funny.'

'My sister's on business in Edinburgh so she won't be there, but you can meet my parents and Ben.'

'Ben?'

He grimaced. 'Ah. I should've checked. Are you OK with dogs?'

'I like them. We just never had one when I was little because he would've spent most of his time in kennels.'

'Ben's a spaniel. He's old, he's greedy and he smells.' He smiled. 'We got him the year I took my GCSEs. He used to sleep on my bed. It drove my mum crazy.'

This was a side of him Jane hadn't seen before. Not the loner: a man who was most definitely part of a family.

Would he be like that with their daughter? With her?

She tried not to let herself hope too much.

And although Mitch had reassured her that his parents would be pleased to meet her, she was still worried. Although she rarely went to the seaside, she couldn't enjoy strolling on the beach hand in hand with Mitch: supposing his family didn't like her? Supposing they compared her with Natalie and she just didn't measure up?

Mitch didn't seem to notice that she was quiet. Though he did make her sit down and have a cold drink, after their walk.

And then it was time to meet his family.

Her heart was beating so hard, so fast, she was sure they must be able to hear it.

'Jane, this is my mum, Elaine, and my dad, George. Mum, Dad—this is Jane.'

Diffidently, Jane held out her hand. 'Pleased to meet you,' she said.

Elaine didn't take her hand. Instead, she gave Jane a warm, welcoming hug. 'And we're so pleased to meet you, Jane. Come and sit down.'

As far as she knew, Mitch hadn't said a word to his parents about her before today, let alone the baby. And yet there was no reserve, no disapproval, no questioning—just acceptance and warmth.

Jane swallowed hard.

'Are you all right, love?' Elaine asked.

'Hormones,' Jane said, hearing the wobble in her voice and hating it. 'I'm sorry. I'm not usually this wet.'

And that was it. The ice was broken. Elaine had tears in her eyes when she saw the photographs of the baby—even more so when Mitch promised to do copies for her. She allowed Jane into her kitchen, but wouldn't let her actually do anything. 'Which isn't because I'm territorial about my kitchen.'

'Being a domestic science teacher, you couldn't be,' Jane said with a smile.

Elaine blinked. 'Mitch told you that?'

'Just before he proved that he could cook as well as I can. He said you taught him.'

Elaine looked pleased, then worry crossed her expression. 'You should be sitting with your feet up. Mitch said you're only just out of bed after a scare.' She looked grim. 'If he'd told us about you sooner, I could've come up to give you a hand.'

'I'm sorry about that.'

Elaine smiled ruefully and hugged her again. 'It's not you, love. It's him. But he's spoken more to us today than he has in the previous year—which I think is down to you. It's been a rough couple of years.' She paused. 'Do you know about…?'

'Natalie?' Jane nodded. 'And I'm not trying to take her place. I'm just me.'

'I know that, love. And I'm looking forward to getting to know you.' Elaine smiled at her. 'I promise I'm not going to be one of these interfering mothers-in-law. But I'd like to think I could come up and see you from time to time.'

'I'd love that,' Jane said, meaning it. 'We could have lunch.'

'And a spa day.'

Things Jane sometimes wished she could share with her own mother. 'That'd be really nice.'

'So are you going back to work after the baby?'

'We haven't discussed that.' Jane decided not to tell Mitch's mother that her son had refused to discuss anything to do with the baby until today. 'But I'd like to go back part-time, at least. I love my job, and I think it'll be good for the baby if I keep up my non-baby interests.'

'What do you do? Mitch didn't say.'

'I'm a record office archivist,' Jane told her.

'Sounds interesting.'

Jane laughed. '*Some* people think it's boring, being stuck in one place with a pile of old documents.'

'Some people,' Elaine said, smiling, 'are far more boring when they start talking about coefficients and vectors and wind-speeds. Don't listen to him. Tell me more about what you do.'

Encouraged, Jane explained more about her job.

'You know, I've always thought about researching the history of this house,' Elaine said. 'It's one of the oldest in the village. I keep saying I'm going to start a project one summer holidays, but I've never got round to it.'

'I could help, if you like,' Jane offered.

'I'd love it.' Elaine smiled. 'And it'd be a good excuse to meet up.'

'You don't need an excuse. I'm just so...well, relieved,' Jane admitted. 'With Mitch not telling you anything about me, I thought you might...'

'Not accept you?' Elaine guessed. 'You've taken away some of the shadows in his eyes. He's not an easy man, and there will be times when you want to throttle him. But it's clear to me in the way you look at him that you love him. And that's enough for me.' Elaine hugged her. 'Now, stop it, or you'll have me in tears, too!'

Love.

That was when it really hit Jane.

Mitch hadn't told her he loved her. But *she* hadn't said it to *him*, either.

And she did love him.

Even when he was being impossible and closed off.

She couldn't pinpoint the exact moment that physical attraction had turned into liking, let alone where liking had blurred into love. But over the last few months—even though he drove her crazy, at times—she'd fallen for him. And she knew it was the for-ever kind of love. The sort that wouldn't go away.

But as for telling him...she'd have to pick her time carefully. A time when he'd be receptive instead of sticking another wall up.

'Your parents are lovely,' Jane said to Mitch as he drove back to London. 'And you don't know how lucky you are, having a family who are settled.'

He frowned. 'I thought you didn't have any hang-ups about your family.'

'I don't. But it'd just be nice to see them more often than I do. Half the time I have no idea where they are, beyond a vague location such as "Turkey".' She shrugged. 'Still, I suppose at least our baby will see a decent amount of one set of grandparents.'

Mitch reached over to squeeze her hand. 'So what did your parents say when you told them?'

Oh, so he was going to ask, then? 'Not much.' Jane

shrugged. 'They were pleased. But they're pretty wrapped up in their work.'

As Mitch was. She really hoped that Mitch wouldn't follow in their footsteps and be too busy for his daughter. But they'd just have to take it step by step.

CHAPTER TWELVE

THE two half-days at the end of the week helped Jane ease back into work. She loved being back in the archives, even though her boss Stella fussed over her and barely let her lift so much as a piece of paper.

'Look, I'm not going to do anything risky. I'll make someone else get the tithe maps or boxes of manorial records out, and I won't go up any ladders. Believe me, after spending a week stuck in bed, no way will I risk anything that'll put me back there again,' Jane said feelingly.

'Hmm. Does Hannah know you're here?' Stella asked, eyes narrowed.

'Yes. And she and Mitch and Charlie and Shelley have already read me the Riot Act. So I'll take it as read, from you.' Jane smiled to take the sting from her words.

'If you feel even the slightest bit rough, you stop work and go home immediately,' Stella said. 'Understood?'

'Understood.'

'Good.' Stella smiled at her. 'So is Mitch going to stick around, now?'

'I hope so.' She really hoped so. And now that he'd bonded with the baby, there was no need for him to run away—was there?

He met her from work at lunchtime, and she enjoyed walking hand in hand with him along the river before having a light lunch and heading home. He seemed more settled, now. Although he still hadn't gone shopping with her for baby things—he was still insisting that she took more rest than she thought she needed—she felt he'd finally accepted the baby. He'd finally accepted that the future was going to happen, that it was time to move on.

And Jane was relaxed enough to start making plans on the Monday night, on the way home from work on the tube. She was still daydreaming when she unlocked the front door.

'Honey, I'm ho-ome,' she called. If he made any comment, she'd say she was being ironic. But she loved the feeling of coming home to him. Of knowing that he was here. Of knowing she was *home*.

'I'm in here,' he called back.

She walked towards the bedroom—and stopped dead in the doorway when she saw what he was doing.

'Why are you packing?'

'Because you're a lot better now, you're back at work full-time, and I have a project that's seriously close to missing its deadline.'

'You're going away again.' Clearly she'd been fooling herself. But after the time they'd shared, the way they'd bonded during her sick leave, the way he'd started talking about their baby, the fact he'd taken her to meet his family…she'd been so sure he would stay, this time.

He sat on the edge of the bed. 'Jane, this is what I do. You know that. It's how I earn my living. If I keep taking time off, we're going to be living on dry bread and water.'

She lifted her chin. 'I have a job. I'm perfectly capable of paying my half of the bills.'

'I know you are. But this is who I am, Jane. I'm a stormchaser.'

'Mmm-hmm.' She willed the tears to stay back—no way was she going to let him see her crying over this.

'I'll be back.'

'As soon as. Yeah, I know.' She forced herself to smile outwardly—but inside she wasn't smiling. 'So I guess I'm not going to get to see you off at the airport.' Again.

'That's fine.'

No, it wasn't. But suddenly she was just too tired to argue the point.

By Friday, Mitch was chain-drinking coffee.

This was ridiculous.

He loved his job. And he had plenty to do, given that he'd needed to take unscheduled time off to look after Jane. So why wasn't he enjoying his work, the way he used to? Where was the adrenalin rush when he looked at the screen and saw the weather systems moving, storms forming? Why did this all feel so...unimportant?

'So how are things?' Brad came to sit beside him and proffered an open bag of doughnuts.

Even the sugar rush didn't help. 'Fine,' Mitch lied.

'At home, I meant. Jane's all right? And the baby?'

To Mitch's relief, Brad had kept his voice low so nobody else on the team could hear. Even though Mitch had seen the baby for himself at the scan, knew everything was going to be all right, he still felt it was tempting fate to announce the news to everyone, the way he had with Natalie. 'They're both fine, thanks. We had a scan last week.' He paused. 'We're having a little girl.'

'Got any pictures?'

Ha. If anyone had told him six months ago that he'd be showing baby pictures to a colleague, Mitch would've considered having them certified insane. But here he was, taking his mobile phone out of his pocket and flicking into the screen where he'd emailed the pictures from the scan. 'Here.'

'Wow—that's incredible. They didn't have this sort of thing when my kids were small. Just the grainy black and white blob that you told everyone was a baby and you could say where the head was and maybe an arm or leg, but that was it. This is...wow.'

'The technology's pretty amazing,' Mitch agreed.

'And your mind isn't here at all, is it?'

'I love what I do,' Mitch protested, 'and I'm committed to the project.'

'Nobody's questioning that. But you haven't taken a single picture today,' Brad pointed out quietly.

'No,' Mitch admitted. 'I love all this. So I don't understand why it's…' He sighed and took another bite of doughnut. 'It's dragging.'

'That's because you're missing home. Missing Jane. Missing the baby,' Brad said, patting his shoulder. 'And it'll get worse when the babe arrives. Kids grow up really quickly, you know. My youngest starts high school next term and it doesn't seem like a blink of an eye since the eldest was in preschool.'

'Yeah.' Mitch finished his doughnut. 'We'd better get some work done.'

'Sure.'

But the empty feeling didn't go away. And whereas he'd never really noticed his surroundings before, now he found himself comparing them with home. Sure, the motel had a comfortable bed and there was nothing to complain about, but it was so impersonal. The room was soulless. Even the picture on the wall was completely bland—the pictures in their flat had the rich colours of a print from a Book of Hours, or fascinating detail in the copies of ancient maps.

He'd spent almost two weeks back with Jane, and in that time he'd grown used to curling round her body at night. Used to the way she fitted so perfectly against him. Used to her warmth. The motel's double bed felt way too wide—and he had a feeling that it would've been just as bad in a single bed.

He didn't belong here any more.

He belonged in London. With Jane. With the woman he loved.

And how long it had taken him to realise that.

He wanted to ring her right there and then—but it was

stupid o'clock in the morning her time, and she really needed her sleep. A text wouldn't do it, either. He wanted to tell her face to face. That finally he was free of his demons. That he loved her.

And he'd ask her to marry him.

He found himself counting the days until he was due home again. The only thing that kept him going was the fact that he'd found the perfect ring. A very plain platinum band with a round-cut solitaire diamond. But not just any diamond: this one was blue. Exactly the same shade of blue as Jane's eyes.

Brad whistled when he saw it. 'That must've set you back quite a few dollars.'

Mitch laughed. 'It's half a carat—not *quite* the Hope Diamond. Besides, natural blue diamonds are rare, so this one's an enhanced one.'

'Even so, I've seen the websites my wife drools over. These babies are seriously expensive. And is that a platinum setting?' Brad held it up to the light. 'Don't you dare tell Deanna or she'll want one and I'll have to take out a second mortgage!' He raised an eyebrow. 'So you're going to ask Jane to marry you?'

'Just as soon as I get home.' Then Mitch's smile faded. 'I just hope she'll say yes.'

Mitch didn't tell Jane when he was coming back, because he wanted to surprise her. He picked up the biggest bouquet of flowers he could find at the airport, then caught the train back to Isleworth.

It seemed oddly quiet when he opened the front door. Jane wasn't one to have the TV on all the time, but she usually had music playing. Maybe she'd gone round to see the girls, he thought. He dropped his suitcase in the hall, closed the door and went to put the flowers in water in the sink until he could give them to her properly—and, more importantly, the velvet-covered box in his pocket.

But something didn't seem right about the kitchen. Something felt…missing. He couldn't quite put his finger on what.

Frowning, he walked into the living room.

And then it hit him.

There were no plants.

No cushions.

His heart missed a beat. No. He was just being paranoid. She wouldn't have…would she?

He went straight to the wardrobe in their bedroom. Opened the doors.

And it was empty, apart from a few hangers rattling on the rail.

He grabbed his phone and called Jane's mobile.

'Where are you?' he asked, without preamble, when she answered it.

'Where are *you*?' she fenced.

'Our flat.'

'Ah.'

'What do you mean, ah?'

'I moved back home.'

'Home?'

'With the girls.'

'I don't believe this,' he muttered through clenched teeth. 'Why? When? And why the hell didn't you tell me what you were going to do?'

'Why is obvious. When—the day after you left. And I didn't tell you because you didn't tell me you were on your way back. I didn't want a long-distance row with you, but I had intended to tell you before you got to the flat.'

She was calling it 'the flat' again, he noticed. Not 'our flat'.

'I don't understand why,' he said. 'We need to talk. I'm coming over.'

'I don't want a fight, Mitch.'

'Neither do I!'

'Then stop shouting at me.'

Was he? He raked a hand through his hair. 'Sorry. I didn't realise I was. It's just… I was looking forward to coming home. To you. And you moved out without even telling me.'

'I'll come over now,' Jane said. 'We'll talk. But I want you to be very clear about one thing: I won't be staying.'

He was still brooding when she rang the bell.

'Why didn't you use your key?' he demanded.

'Because I don't live here any more. But thanks for reminding me.' She rummaged in her handbag, took out her keychain and removed the front-door key; then she handed it back to him. 'Yours.'

'No.' He shook his head. 'It's not meant to be like this. I don't understand what went wrong.'

She sighed. 'Let's sit down.'

'Do you need a drink or anything?'

'I'm fine, thanks.'

He was so tense he could barely sit still. But he managed it. Just. 'So explain to me. I thought everything was OK.'

'I've had a lot of time on my own to think about things. About the baby, about how I want my life to be.' She looked him straight in the eye, and the sheer sadness in her face gave him a pain in the centre of his chest. 'This isn't it, Mitch. I don't want to spend all my time waiting for you to come back from chasing a storm.'

When he was about to protest, she held up a hand. 'Hear me out. You know how I grew up. I love my parents, and I know they love me—but their work always came first. Always. They took Alex and me with them a lot at first, but then they sent us both to boarding-school. And, yes, it made me sensible and self-reliant and all that jazz, and, yes, I'm ridiculously proud of them because they're brilliant—but just sometimes it would've been nice to have a *normal* home. To be a normal teenager, squabbling with my parents over my hair and my clothes and the fact I was wearing way too much make-up and how loudly I played my music. I wanted a normal life with a normal family, Mitch. I still do. And I won't get that with you.'

'Yes, you will.' His hand closed round the velvet box in his pocket.

'Mitch, you say that now. But I know how it is. You'll be here for a while, and then you'll get itchy feet and you'll be off again.' She swallowed hard. 'I'm not going to ask you to give up your job—I know how much it means to you and I know it's who you are. My brother Alex is the same as you—but I'm not. I want to be in one place. I want to be *settled*.' She took a deep breath. 'The baby's the most important thing to me, now. I don't want her to grow up the way I did, either tagging along behind us while you're chasing some storm or other, or stuck at home with me and hating the fact she almost never sees her dad.'

No, no, no. It *wasn't* going to be like that. His grip on the box tightened, but he knew now wasn't the right time to ask her to marry him. Because she'd say no. And he needed her to say yes.

'Jane, of course she'll see me,' Mitch said.

'When you're in the country. Which isn't that much. It's not the same as being a full-time dad, Mitch. I want a proper home for my baby. Somewhere settled. Not running after you, or coping on my own. That's why I moved back with the girls. Having three godmothers around is going to be much better for me and for the baby. I'll have support when I need it. And my baby's going to have all the love she could ask for.'

'You don't have to cope on your own. I'll be here.'

She shook her head. 'You won't. And if you give everything up you'll get bored. You'll miss the adrenalin rush. You'll miss the buzz of chasing the storms and taking your incredible pictures.'

He ignored her, focusing on the rest of her previous statement. 'And I'll give my baby all the love she needs.'

'That's a knee-jerk reaction. It's better this way—better all round. You won't feel tied down or trapped.'

'So what are you saying? That it's over? That I won't see…' his mouth dried '…you or the baby again?'

'No. Of *course* you'll see the baby when you're home. I'd never deny you access. Or your parents—I'd like my baby to know her grandparents, too.' She frowned. 'But if you really want the safety net of a legal agreement I'm happy to sort that out.'

'But, Jane—' He took the box out of his pocket.

She wasn't even looking. 'No buts,' she said quietly. 'I'm doing this because I love you, Mitch.'

She loved him? And she was leaving him because of that? What? That didn't make sense.

'I know that to keep you trapped in one place would make you unhappy. So I'm setting you free. Free to chase your storms and your dreams.' She stood up, walked over to him and kissed him lightly. 'Goodbye, Mitch.'

This couldn't be happening. This wasn't how it was meant to be. He'd intended to give her the flowers, then get down on one knee and tell her he loved her. Ask her to make his life complete by marrying him.

But then the front door closed behind her.

And he still couldn't move a muscle.

CHAPTER THIRTEEN

THIS wasn't what Mitch wanted. At all. But Jane had walked out without even giving him a chance to tell her everything he felt. He hadn't told her that he realised now how much he loved her, that she and the baby were important to him, that he didn't want to be away any more.

More importantly, he hadn't had the chance to ask her to marry him.

He'd tried to tell her.

But she'd refused to believe him. She'd said he'd be bored.

Though he knew he wouldn't.

He wanted to be there, with her. Make the home she wanted. Let their baby grow up in a normal family, just as he had. He wanted to be a lover and a husband and a father. He wanted to make a family with her.

How was he going to get her to believe he was serious? That he really, really meant it?

Telling her wouldn't be enough: he already knew that. He needed to show her. And he'd need more than just the blue diamond to make her believe him.

Despite the jet lag he didn't sleep well that night.

But by the morning he had a plan.

Jane wanted a home. She wanted to be settled.

He'd give her what she wanted.

All wrapped up.

He just needed a hand with the details.

Three phone calls set two of the parts of his plan in motion. The third bit needed some research. And a lot of luck—because he needed this all sorted by Christmas. Which gave him a shade under four months to do this.

He just hoped to hell he was doing the right thing. That it would be enough to convince Jane of how he really felt about her.

He spent the morning on the Internet, browsing properties. By lunchtime, he had a shortlist of six. But when he visited them, none of them was right.

Another week of searching and getting nowhere. Of ringing Jane just to say hello, but she made excuse after excuse not to see him. Seven job interviews—five of which he knew he wouldn't take even if he was offered them, one he'd refused on the spot, and one he really wanted but he'd worked with a couple of the other short-listed candidates and knew they had more experience.

And then things started to click into place. Firstly his own estate agent called him—his tenants wanted to buy the house in Cambridge. At a shade under the asking price, but that was fine by him: the important thing was that he wouldn't be stuck in a chain. He really, really didn't have time for that.

And then a London agency rang him. 'Mr Holland? We've just taken some new instructions that I think might interest you.'

He scribbled down the details. Met the estate agent outside. And the moment he walked inside, he knew it was the right one. Three bedrooms—one for them, one for their daughter, and one for a little brother or sister. A reasonable-sized living room and kitchen diner. A conservatory they could use as a playroom. A garden big enough to mean they could have a dog.

It was the right house. And he'd seen it on the day he'd sold his own property. So this had to be fate. 'I'll pay the full asking price.'

He didn't get the job he'd wanted—but he was grateful, two weeks later, when a job that suited him even more came up.

And a month later, he had the house keys. The whole package.

Almost.

All he needed now was his wife and baby and his life would be complete. Jane was still being difficult about seeing him. 'You said you weren't going to refuse me access,' he pointed out. 'But you're refusing to see me. So, actually, you *are* refusing me access.'

'The baby isn't here yet,' she reminded him.

'I'm missing out on the bump.'

'And you weren't while you were chasing storms?'

He sighed. 'I don't want to fight. I just want to see you. I miss you.'

'Hmm.' But she agreed to see him for lunch.

And he made a point of asking about the baby as well as her, straight off. Though he noticed that she was shifting about a bit in her seat. 'What's up?'

'Someone's practising for the Olympics.'

The baby was kicking? He stared at her T-shirt covered bump, and he could definitely see movement. 'May I?'

She shrugged. 'Sure.'

He placed his hand on her bump. Felt tiny shocks from the baby kicking. And he was so choked he could barely speak. He left his hand where it was for a moment or two after the baby had stopped kicking. God, he'd missed touching her. Maybe if he pulled her into his arms and kissed her stupid, it'd break down the barriers between them and everything would be all right.

But, knowing Jane, it was more likely to make things ten times worse.

So he removed his hand. Kept his libido well in check. And just said softly, 'Thank you.'

Although he was still carrying the ring around with him, now wasn't the time to give it to her. Or the door key that he'd planned to wrap up in a small box with a ribbon round it: until the house was painted and furnished and he could give her the home of her dreams, he didn't want her even guessing of its existence.

So he kept conversation light. Did his best to be charming. Extracted a promise from Jane to meet him every Wednesday. And then persuaded her to make an even more important promise: that she'd let him drive her to hospital and support her through labour. That he could be there when their little girl was born.

Stage two—decorating the house—meant he needed help. Sure, he could do the whole place in neutral tones—but he wanted Jane to walk in and see her dream, not just the potential.

'Why are you ringing me?' Hannah asked the next morning, sounding puzzled.

'Because I've got your number. And I need your help.'

'How do you mean?'

'Meet me for lunch, and I'll explain,' Mitch said. 'Name the time and place, and I'll be there. But I really need your help—and I also need this to be confidential.'

'I don't like the sound of this,' Hannah said.

'It's nothing bad, I promise. But I don't want Jane knowing a thing.'

'I can't promise that.'

'It's nothing bad,' he repeated. 'But—look, just hear me out over lunch, and then make your decision.'

She was silent for a moment, and he thought she was going to say no.

He only realised he'd been holding his breath when she said, 'OK. Wait for me outside the surgery at half past twelve. I might be a few minutes late if my surgery overruns.'

'You,' Mitch said, 'are a wonderful woman. Thank you.' He scribbled down the address she gave him, and at half past twelve precisely he was outside the surgery.

She was ten minutes late.

But, hey, he could wait. If he had Hannah and the girls on his side, this would work out.

They had lunch in a café just down the road. And as soon as they'd ordered a meal, he took the box out of his pocket and showed her the contents.

'A sapphire?' she asked. 'It's very sparkly for a sapphire.'

'That's because it isn't one. It's a blue diamond,' Mitch said. 'I came home with it, intending to ask Jane to marry me—but she'd already moved out.'

Hannah shook her head, clearly exasperated. 'Mitch, she's spent the last few months waiting around for you. The only time you've been there was when it was a real emergency—and even then you had to travel practically halfway across the world, first.'

'It's going to change,' Mitch said. 'I've told her that, but I know that words aren't enough. I need to prove to her that I mean it. And that means making her a proper home.' He smiled at her. 'Which is where you come in. I need inside information. The kind of colours she likes, the kind of furniture.'

'Wait a minute. What do you mean, a proper home?'

'The house of her dreams.'

'You've actually bought a house?'

'A couple of roads away from you,' Mitch confirmed. 'So if Jane wants to go back to work, she'll still have an easy journey in; if she doesn't want to go back to work, she's near playgroups and what have you; and she's not far away from you, Charlie and Shelley.' He paused. 'If you want to check it out…'

'Not just me. Charlie and Shelley.'

'Sure, but don't do it all at the same time or she'll get suspicious. Oh, and it smells of paint at the moment.'

'You're painting the house?'

'In the evenings when I'm home from work.'

'Which is where? Outer Mongolia?'

Mitch sighed. 'London. It's a desk job but still in the same field as my old job. And it's flexible—I can work from home, some of the time.'

'Let me get this straight. You've bought a house and you've got a job in London.'

'And I've bought the safest family car on the market,' he added.

She shook her head. 'You're the man who lives out of a suitcase, drives a flash car and never stays in the same place longer than about a week.'

'Not any more,' he said softly. 'All I need to do is persuade Jane to marry me.'

'And if she says no?'

'Then I resort to nagging,' Mitch said, 'until she says yes. So are you going to help me?'

'Decorate?'

'Not unless you want to pick up a paintbrush.' He smiled. 'Actually, slapping paint on the walls is pretty relaxing. But then again, if you go home smelling of paint or with bits in your hair, she might guess, and I don't want her knowing about it until the house is ready. Just how she wants it. So if you want to stick to being my style consultant, that's fine.'

'Charlie's our style queen,' Hannah said, sounding doubtful. 'You might be better asking her.'

'Charlie's scary. And you were the one who rang me when Jane needed me. I trust you.' He slid a file across the table. 'Catalogues. Including nursery furniture. Get her to look through them, then tell me the ones she likes.' He handed her a card. 'You know my mobile number. This is work.'

She glanced at the card, then stared at him. 'You're serious.'

'I'm absolutely serious,' he said. 'I'm settling. But until Jane's there with me, the house is never going to be home.'

'OK. I'm in,' Hannah said. 'And I can speak for Charlie and Shelley as well.'

'And you'll keep it to yourselves?'

She nodded. 'If you're working this hard to give her the home of her dreams—changing your life to put her at the centre—then you love her. And you're going to take care of her. So, yes.'

A month later, Mitch walked from room to room, looking at each one in turn as he leant against the door jambs.

Perfect.

Clean, fresh colours on the walls that made the most of the light. Curtains in toning shades—thanks to Hannah's mum, who'd given him detailed instructions on how to measure up and what to buy, and then came round to press out the creases and help him hang the material from the plain but stylish curtain rods he'd chosen. Carpets with a subtle fleck so the place wouldn't look as if it needed vacuuming again five minutes after it had been done. Some of his photographs, framed, on the walls—and spaces he planned to fill with photographs of their baby. Furniture, thanks to Hannah, Charlie and Shelley, who'd vetted the house, declared their approval, and met him secretly for lunch with his pile of catalogues marked with the kind of things Jane liked.

And the nursery.

He'd painted it in the softest shade of yellow, then hand-painted a frieze of swimming ducklings around the walls just above the top of the crib. It had taken him ages. And although several times he'd been at the point of just painting the whole thing over and buying a paper frieze instead to cover up the mess, he'd persisted.

He just hoped Jane liked the finished result.

Home.

Where he'd be happy to settle.

Where his heart was. Or would be, once Jane and the baby moved in too.

He went back down to the kitchen and took a small box and a reel of ribbon from a carrier bag. All he had to do now was wrap Jane's Christmas present.

The key to their home.

And hope that in three weeks' time she understood exactly what he was giving her.

CHAPTER FOURTEEN

A WEEK later, Mitch was in the office, up to his eyes in figures, charts and maps, when the phone rang.

He answered it absently. 'Mitch Holland.'

'It's becoming a bit of a habit, this,' Hannah said dryly. 'Ringing you and telling you that Jane's in hospital.'

'What?' He snapped to full attention. 'Oh, my God. She isn't having another abruption, is she?'

'No. She's in labour. Her waters broke.'

'It's four weeks too early! She *can't* be in labour yet.'

'Don't panic.' Hannah was using her soft, professional voice—and that scared him even more. Was she telling him not to panic because something was wrong?

'Lots of babies arrive early and they do just fine,' she said.

And some of them didn't.

And she'd already had that scare earlier in her pregnancy.

Mitch went cold. 'I'm on my way.' He banged down the receiver, left everything else where it was on his desk, and put his head round his boss's door. 'I have to go. My…' Ah, hell. How did he explain what Jane was? 'My other half's in labour and her best friend's just taken her to hospital.'

His boss stared at him in shock. 'What? I didn't even know you were—'

'It's complicated and it's messy and I'm sorry I haven't explained before. I'll fill you in as soon as I can. But right now I need to be with Jane,' Mitch cut in. 'I haven't switched anything off—if someone could…?' He swallowed hard. Every second he was wasting here was a second where he should be supporting Jane.

'Don't worry about things here,' his boss said, still looking stunned but clearly thinking on his feet. 'Good luck. Let us know how things go.'

'Thanks. I will.'

And then Mitch was running out of the building.

What was the fastest way to get to the hospital?

The tube would take too long—whether he went back to the house and picked up his car, or changed from the tube to the overland rail network to get to the hospital. No way was he going to sit while a bus chugged from stop to stop—not that he knew which number bus he needed anyway.

'Taxi!' he yelled.

At the third attempt, he managed to flag one down. As soon as he explained he needed to get to the hospital because his partner was in labour, the cabbie nodded and took off through the back streets.

It wasn't meant to be like this.

Jane was meant to wake up with labour pains, call him, and he'd go over to her place, distract her until the contractions were five minutes apart, and then he'd drive her to the hospital himself.

But their baby had clearly had other ideas.

He grabbed his mobile and punched in the number of Jane's mobile phone.

It was switched off.

He dragged in a breath. Of course it would be. You were supposed to switch your mobile phone off in hospital. Where was his brain—outer space?

Oh, God. Please let her be all right. Please let their baby be all right. Please don't let this all go wrong.

Every second of the journey—despite the fact that the cabbie wasn't sticking strictly to the speed limits—felt like an hour.

And finally they were there.

Mitch glanced at the display showing the fare, took some notes from his wallet and thrust them into the cabbie's hand. 'Thanks, mate. Keep the change.'

And then he ran through the hospital, not slowing until he reached the maternity department.

'Jane Redmond, please. I'm her partner,' he said at the reception desk.

The midwife checked on the screen. 'She's in Delivery Suite Two. Come through.'

The fact he had to walk instead of run in the hospital gave him time to think.

Time to remember.

And he felt physically sick.

His breath hitched. What had happened with Natalie wasn't going to happen with Jane. He wasn't going to lose her—or the baby. Everything was going to be just fine. And for Jane's sake he really had to get a grip.

Right now.

When the midwife showed him into the delivery suite, Jane was sitting on the bed with Hannah in the chair by her side. Jane was wired up to various machines, looking white-faced and terrified.

He was just as terrified, but he knew she needed him to be strong. He slid his arms round her and held her close, stroked her hair. 'Hey. Everything's going to be fine. We're in the right place so there's nothing to worry about. We can do this.' He looked at Hannah. 'Thanks for being here. And for calling me.'

'No worries,' Hannah said. 'This is Rebecca, Jane's midwife.'

'You're Jane's partner?' Rebecca asked.

Because Jane was letting him hold her, he took the risk that she wouldn't correct him. 'Yes—I'm Mitch. Can you tell me what's happening, please?'

'Because Jane's waters have broken, we're monitoring the baby. Everything's fine. We could wait and see if Jane goes into labour naturally—which most women do within a day or so of their waters breaking—but that does carry a risk of infection.'

Mitch had to stem the surge of panic. He wasn't going to lose Jane. Not now.

'But given the abruption earlier in the pregnancy, Jane's agreed that we should induce the labour. We're giving her a drug called oxytocin—'

'Through a drip, to help the contractions?' he finished, on familiar ground now.

The midwife smiled at him. 'Sounds as if you've been reading up.'

'On everything,' Mitch agreed.

Jane stared at him. 'Since when?'

'You'd be surprised.' And thank God he'd finished painting the house and putting the furniture together.

She dragged in a breath. 'I'm scared.'

So was he, but he stroked Jane's forehead, soothing her. 'It's going to be fine. Trust me, honey.'

'But the baby's too early.'

'Lots of babies are born at thirty-six weeks.' He glanced at Rebecca for reassurance.

'Your baby might need a little while in Special Care to help him or her breathe, but that's very common and nothing to worry about. We can also give you steroids to help mature the baby's lungs. But everything's fine on the monitor,' Rebecca said.

'Now you're here, Mitch, I'd better go to work,' Hannah said.

'Sure. Thanks again for coming to the rescue. Did you bring the hospital bag?'

'I hadn't packed it yet,' said Jane. 'I was going to do that next week.' She swallowed hard. 'It's my first day of maternity leave today and this wasn't supposed to happen!'

'I know.' He wiped the tears away with the pad of his thumb.

'But we're here now. Everything's going to be fine. I can get you whatever you need from the hospital shop.'

'Better than that,' Hannah said, 'I'll tell Charlie what you need, and get her to pack the bag for you.'

But although Jane's waters had broken, the baby seemed to have no intention of coming out. Mitch stayed with her, not wanting to leave her even for long enough to buy a sandwich. And he held her hand, wiped her face with a wet cloth, held a cup for her to sip water, and rubbed her back when the contractions grew more painful.

Finally, the obstetrician came in and examined Jane. 'I'm afraid labour's not progressing, Mrs Redmond, and the baby's starting to show signs of distress. We need to take you to theatre for a Caesarean section.'

Jane's face went white and she gripped Mitch's hand. 'Don't leave me.'

'Of course I won't.' He kissed her forehead. 'It's going to be OK. Half an hour and we're going to meet our baby.'

Even though his legs felt shaky with panic, he forced himself to look calm and followed the midwife to don a gown and mask and scrub up.

He held Jane's hand all the way through the operation. Finally, the surgeon took the baby out—and there was silence in the room.

A silence that ripped his heart out.

Please, please, don't let this be happening. Don't let it all go wrong.

And then—after what could only have been seconds but which felt like hours—there was a cry.

'Congratulations,' the surgeon said. 'You have a little girl. Would you like to cut the cord, Mr Redmond?'

Mitch didn't bother correcting his name. Their baby was more important. He just smiled, and held Jane's hand a little tighter. 'May I?' he asked her softly.

She nodded. He cut the cord and held their daughter while Jane was stitched up.

'She needs a little bit of help breathing at the moment, so we need to take her to Special Care,' Rebecca told them, 'but it's very, very common with babies born at thirty-six weeks. She's looking very well, so there's nothing to worry about.'

But it felt strange, going back to the ward without their baby.

Jane looked exhausted, and was clearly close to tears.

'I'm staying,' Mitch said. 'Go to sleep. There's nothing to worry about because I'm here. And we'll tell everyone the news tomorrow.'

When Jane woke, early the following morning, Mitch was dozing in the chair next to her.

He looked rough.

Seriously rough.

His clothes—which he'd worn for a day and a night—were creased, he needed a shave, and there were deep shadows under his eyes.

Her eyes brimmed with tears. He probably hadn't slept; the chair didn't look particularly comfortable. But he'd insisted on staying, being there for her.

Dared she hope it would last?

But she'd seen the wanderlust in her parents, in her brothers. Mitch would be miserable if he didn't chase storms. He'd feel trapped. And little by little, day by day, he'd start to resent her.

It would be better to stop things here. Try and manage on her own.

Even looking a mess, he was the most gorgeous man she'd ever seen.

But she really couldn't let her heart rule her head on this one. For her baby's sake.

When he finally woke, he focused on her. 'Jane. How are you feeling?'

'Fine.' She ached, but she wasn't going to tell him that. 'Look—you really ought to go and get some proper sleep. I can manage here.'

'I'm not leaving you.'

'I can manage.'

'I'm not disputing that. But last night I saw my baby take her first breath. I'm not going anywhere.'

Meaning that it was the baby he wanted, not her? 'I think you'd better leave.'

He sighed. 'You've been through a lot so now isn't the time for a fight—but you and I are going to sit down and have a serious, serious talk. Very soon. And I'll call Hannah and get one of them to come over and be with you.'

Mitch left—but wasn't gone for that long. He visited her every single day, and as soon as their daughter was out of the special care unit he spent most of the time in Jane's room cuddling the baby. And the tenderness in his face made her want to cry.

She couldn't take his daughter away from him.

But she didn't want to be second-best, either. She'd already spent too much of her life feeling second-best—trying to put a brave face on it and not seem as if she minded, but she did mind. A lot.

Finally, they were allowed home. And although Jane had intended to take a taxi, Mitch insisted on driving her himself.

She frowned as he parked the car. 'This is the wrong road.'

'Nope.'

Oh, no. Was he intending to have this heart-to-heart with her right now? 'You can't park here. This is a permit parking zone.'

'I know. And it's fine.'

How?

Before she could argue, he took a box from his pocket and handed it to her. 'Here.'

'What's this?'

'Your Christmas present. A week early.' He smiled. 'Just like you gave me mine a bit earlier.'

'Christmas present?'

He sighed. 'Just open it.'

She undid the ribbon around the flat box, wondering what on earth this was. It wasn't the right shape for a ring.

And then she opened it. Saw a key attached to a keyring.

'It's the front door,' Mitch said. 'I'll give you the back-door key later.' He got out of the car and unstrapped the baby's car seat. 'Come on. It's going to start raining any minute and I don't want Chloë getting cold.'

Still not understanding, she followed him down the path. 'What's this about?' she asked.

'We're home,' he said softly, and stood aside. 'Unlock the door.'

She did, and he carried the baby inside; then he returned, lifted her up and carried her over the threshold.

She stared around in amazement. 'This is your house?'

'No. Ours,' he corrected.

'But...'

'I've been painting for weeks,' he said with a smile. 'Come and have a look round.' He ushered her into the living room. There was a huge Christmas tree in the corner, decorated with lights and baubles and with a pile of wrapped presents beneath it. The baby, in her rocking seat, was sleeping peacefully next to the tree.

Jane walked through to the dining room and then to the kitchen in silence.

It was amazing.

Mitch had made her the home she would've made for herself.

A tear slid down her cheek, and he wiped it away with the pad of his thumb. 'Don't cry, honey. If you don't like it, tell me what you want and I'll change it.'

Don't like it? She *loved* it. 'You've done all this for me?' she asked, hearing the wobble in her voice.

'I thought I'd show you how much I love you,' he said softly. 'This is it. Home. I've got a job in London, and the hours are flexible so I can work round whatever you want to do.' He took a business card from his pocket and gave it to her. 'See? My office isn't that far from here. I can pick our little girl up from nursery or school if you want to go back to work.'

He'd changed his life completely for her?

'Come and see upstairs.'

The nursery had her in tears again. He'd picked the exact furniture she'd wanted. 'You did all this yourself?'

'Well—apart from the curtains. I admit Hannah's mum helped there.'

'Hannah knew about this?'

He winced. 'Um. Yeah. Actually, you might as well know the rest of it. Charlie and Shelley helped, too. Guidance on the details—like colour schemes.'

'You plotted all this with the girls.'

'No. I'd already decided that the only way I could show you I was serious about you was to get a proper job and make us a home. They helped me with the details.'

'But—you're a stormchaser.'

'Was. Last time I came home, it was to tell you something. That I need you a hell of a lot more than I need the storms. That the time drags without you. That I missed you so much it hurt. I just wanted to be home, with you.'

'Really?'

'Really.'

'But aren't you going to get bored?'

'No. I'm doing blue-sky work in my new job. And there are always holidays. Where I can take you to see the Northern Lights or a tornado or rainbows across waterfalls—because you're not the sort who'd want to sit on a beach and do nothing all day.'

'Not my kind of holiday,' she admitted.

'You'd be wanting to fossick around the nearest church or

ancient monument or talk your way into the library of some stately home. Which is fine by me. I can still take pictures of skies.' He took her hand and kissed the backs of her fingers. 'Come and see the rest of the house.'

There were two more bedrooms: one quite plain, and the other peaceful and feminine. Both, she noted, contained double beds.

'This is my room?' she asked, gesturing to the feminine one.

'*Our* room—and this is a bridal bed,' Mitch said.

And then he shocked her even more by dropping down on one knee. 'We seem to do everything out of sequence, so let's continue the tradition. You've had our baby, I've carried you over the threshold...so now I think it's time I asked you to marry me.'

'Marry you?'

'Because I love you, Jane. And I want to be with you for the rest of my life. You, me, Chloë—and maybe a little brother or sister. If we're lucky.'

'You love me.'

He pulled the velvet-covered box out of his pocket. 'I bought you this before I came home from the last tornado. And I've been carrying it around with me ever since, waiting for the right time. I love you, Jane Redmond. My life isn't complete without you. Will you marry me?'

She opened the box to find the most beautiful solitaire stone. It sparkled enough to be a diamond; though maybe that was because tears were shimmering her view, because diamonds weren't blue.

She must have said some of it aloud, because he replied, 'This one is.'

'A blue diamond?'

'I noticed it in the shop window. The same colour as your eyes.'

'And you've been carrying it around for months.'

'Mmm-hmm. While I worked out how to show you I meant it. That I love you, and it wasn't just a knee-jerk reaction to you saying that you loved me. That I wanted to make a proper home for the three of us. So do you believe me, now? Will you marry me?'

'Yes, I believe you.' She slid her arms round his neck. Held him really close. 'And, yes, I'll marry you.'

'There are three little words missing,' he reminded her.

She laughed. 'Four. I love you too.'

'Good.' He took the ring from the box, kissed the ring finger of her left hand, then slid the ring onto it. 'The perfect fit,' he said softly. 'Just like our life's going to be.'

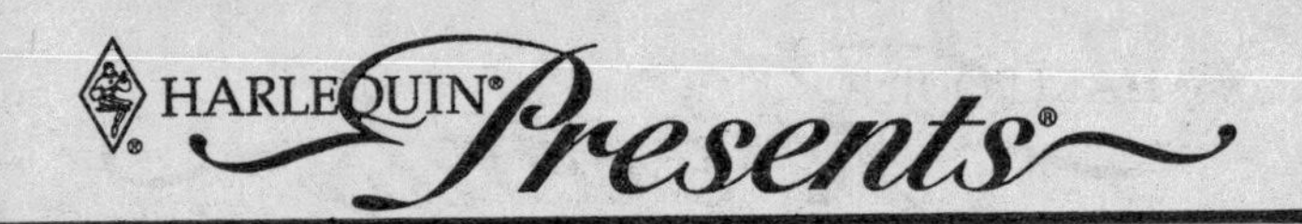

They seek passion—at any price!

Three Sicilians of aristocratic birth—with revenge in mind and romance in their destinies!

Darci intends to teach legendary womanizer Luc Gambrelli a lesson—but as soon as the smolderingly handsome Sicilian film producer turns the tables on her, the game begins to get dirty....

THE SICILIAN'S INNOCENT MISTRESS

The third book in this sizzling trilogy by

Carole Mortimer

Book #2758

Available in September

AN INNOCENT IN HIS BED

He's a man who takes whatever he pleases—even if it means bedding an inexperienced young woman….

With his intense good looks, commanding presence and unquestionable power, he'll carefully charm her and entice her into his bed, where he'll teach her the ways of love—by giving her the most amazingly sensual night of her life!

Don't miss any of the exciting stories in September:

#21 THE CATTLE BARON'S VIRGIN WIFE
by LINDSAY ARMSTRONG

#22 THE GREEK TYCOON'S INNOCENT MISTRESS
by KATHRYN ROSS

#23 PREGNANT BY THE ITALIAN COUNT
by CHRISTINA HOLLIS

#24 ANGELO'S CAPTIVE VIRGIN
by INDIA GREY

www.eHarlequin.com

HPE0908